ROSAMUNDE PILCHER

**A WRITER WHOSE BOOKS ARE
CHERISHED BY READERS TODAY
AND DESTINED TO BE
CLASSICS TOMORROW**

The
DAY
OF THE
STORM

ROSAMUNDE
PILCHER

A DELL BOOK

Published by
Dell Publishing
a division of
Bantam Doubleday Dell Publishing Group, Inc.
1540 Broadway
New York, New York 10036

The trademark Dell® is registered in the U.S. Patent and Trademark Office.

ISBN: 0-440-20253-1

Reprinted by arrangement with St. Martin's Press, Inc.

Printed in the United States of America

May 1989

20 19 18

RAD

1

It all started on a Monday at the end of January. A dull day at a dull time of the year. Christmas and the New Year were over and forgotten and yet the new season had not started to show its face. London was cold and raw, the shops filled with empty hope and clothes "for cruising". The trees in the park stood lacy and bare against low skies, the trodden grass beneath them dull and dead, so that it was impossible to believe that it could ever again be carpeted with drifts of purple and yellow crocus.

It was a day like any other day. The alarm woke me to darkness, but a darkness made paler by the wide expanse of the uncurtained windows, and through them I could see the top of the plane tree, illuminated by the orange glow of distant street lights.

My room was unfurnished, except for the sofa bed on which I lay, and a kitchen table which I was going to strip of paint when I had the time, and polish with a coat of beeswax. Even the floor was bare, boards stretching to the wainscotting. An orange box did duty as a bedside table, and a second one filled in for a chair.

I put out a hand and turned on the light and surveyed the desolate scene with the utmost satisfaction. It was mine. My first home. I had moved in only three weeks ago but it belonged entirely to me. With it, I could do as I pleased. Cover the white walls with posters or paint them orange. Sand the bare floor or stripe it in colour. Already I had started to acquire a proprietary interest in junk and antique shops, and could not pass one without scanning the window for some treasure that I might be able to afford. This was how the table had come into my possession, and I already had my eye on an antique gilt mirror, but had not yet plucked up the courage to go into the shop and find out how much it was going to cost. Perhaps I would hang it in the centre of the chimney breast, or on the wall opposite the window, so that the reflections of the sky and the tree would be caught, like a picture, within its ornate frame.

These pleasant imaginings took some time. I looked again at the clock, saw that it was growing late, and climbed out of bed to pad, barefooted, across the floor and into the tiny kitchen, where I lit the gas and put the kettle on to boil. The day had begun.

The flat was in Fulham, the top floor of a small terrace house which belonged to Maggie and John Trent. I had met them only at Christmas, which I had spent with Stephen Forbes and his wife Mary and their large family of untidy children, in their large and untidy house in Putney. Stephen Forbes was my boss, the owner of the Walton Street bookshop where I had been working for the past year. He had always been enormously kind and helpful towards me and when he found out, from one of the other girls, that I would be on my own for Christmas, he and Mary had immediately issued a firm invitation—more an order, really—that I should spend the three days with them. There was plenty of space, he insisted vaguely, a room in the attic, a bed in Samantha's room, some-where, but I wouldn't mind, would I? And I could always help Mary baste the turkey and pick all those torn bits of tissue paper off the floor.

Considering it from this angle, I finally accepted, and had a wonderful time. There's nothing like a family Christmas when there are children everywhere and noise and paper and presents, and a pine-smell-ing Christmas tree, glittering with baubles and crooked home-made decorations.

On Boxing Night, with the children safely in bed, the Forbeses threw a grown-up party, although we still seemed to continue playing childish games, and Maggie and John Trent came to this. The Trents were young marrieds, she the daughter of an Oxford don, whom Stephen had known well in his under-graduate days. She was one of those laughing, cheer-ful out-going people, and after she had arrived the party went with a swing. We were introduced but we didn't manage to talk until a game of charades, when we found ourselves side by side on a sofa, trying to guess, from the most incoherent gestures, that Mary was trying to act to us, in dumb show, the title of a film. *"Rose Marie!"* somebody yelled, for no apparent reason.

"Clockwork Orange!"

Maggie lit a cigarette and sank back on the sofa, defeated. "It's beyond me," she said. She turned her dark head to look at me. "You work in Stephen's shop, don't you?"

"Yes."

"I'll come in next week and spend all my Christmas book tokens. I've been given dozens."

"Lucky girl."

"We've just moved into our first house, so I want lots of coffee table stuff so that all our friends think I'm wildly intelligent . . ." Then somebody shouted, "Maggie, it's your turn," and she said "Cripes," and shot to her feet, and went stalking off to find out what she was going to have to act. I can't remember what it was, but watching her make a cheerful fool of herself, my heart warmed to her, and I hoped that I would see her again.

I did, of course. True to her word, she came into the shop a couple of days after the holiday wearing a sheepskin coat and a long purple skirt, and carrying a bulging handbag stuffed with book tokens. I wasn't serving anybody at that particular moment and I came out from behind a neat stack of shiny-jacketed novels and said, "Hallo."

"Oh, good, there you are. I was hoping I'd find you. Can you help me?"

"Yes, of course."

Together, we chose a cookery book, a new auto-biography which everybody was talking about, and a marvellously expensive volume of Impressionist paintings for the legendary coffee table. All this came to a little more than the book tokens did, so she groped around in that handbag and took out a cheque book in order to pay for the balance of the amount.

"John'll be furious," she told me happily, writing out the amount with a red felt pen. The cheque was yellow and the effect quite gay. "He says we're spending far too much money as it is. There." She turned it over to write her address. "Fourteen Bracken Road, SW6." She said it aloud in case I couldn't read her writing. "I haven't got used to writing it yet. We've only just moved in. Terribly exciting, we've bought it freehold, believe it or not. At least our parents chipped in with the deposit and John managed to con some building society or other into giving us a loan for the rest. But of course because of this, we've got to let the top floor to help pay the mortgage, but still, I suppose it'll all work out." She smiled. "You'll have to come and see it."

"I'd like to." I was wrapping her parcel, being meticulous about matching the paper and folding the corners.

She watched me. "You know, it's terribly rude,

but I don't know your name. I know it's Rebecca, but Rebecca what?"

"Rebecca Bayliss."

"I suppose you don't know of a nice peaceful individual who wants an unfurnished flat?"

I looked at her. Our thoughts were so close I scarcely had to speak. I tied the knot on the parcel and snapped the string. I said, "How about me?"

"You? But are you looking for somewhere to live?"

"I wasn't until a moment ago. But I am now."

"It's only a room and a kitchen. And we have to share the bath."

"I don't mind if you don't. And if I can afford the rent. I don't know what you're asking."

Maggie told me. I swallowed and did a few mental calculations and said, "I could manage that."

"Have you got any furniture?"

"No. I've been living in a furnished flat with a couple of other girls. But I can get some."

"You sound as though you're desperate to get out."

"No, I'm not desperate, but I'd like to be on my own."

"Well, before you decide you'd better come and see it. Some evening, because John and I both work."

"*This* evening?" It was impossible to keep my impatience and excitement out of my voice and Maggie laughed.

"All right," she said. "This evening," and she

picked up the beautifully wrapped parcel of books and prepared to depart.

I suddenly panicked . . . "I . . . I don't know the address . . ."

"Yes you do, silly, it's on the back of the cheque. Get a twenty-two bus. I'll expect you about seven."

"I'll be there," I promised.

Jolting slowly down the Kings Road in the bus I had to consciously damp down my enthusiasm. I was out to buy a pig in a poke. The flat might be totally impossible, too big, too small or inconvenient in some unimagined way. Anything was better than being disappointed. And indeed, from the outside, the little house was entirely unremarkable, one of a row of red brick villas, with fancy pointing around the doors and a depressing tendency towards stained glass. But inside Number 14 was bright with fresh paint and new carpets and Maggie herself in old jeans and a blue sweater.

"Sorry I look such a mess but I've got to do all the housework, so I usually change when I get back from the office. Come on, let's go up and see it . . . put your coat on the banisters, John's not home yet, but I told him you were coming and he thought it was a frightfully good idea . . ."

Talking all the time, she led the way upstairs and into the empty room which stood at the back of the house. She turned on the light. "It faces south, out over a little park. The people who had the house before us built an extension on underneath, so you've got a sort of balcony on its roof." She opened a glass door and we stepped together out into the cold dark night, and I smelt the leaf-smell of the park, and damp earth, and saw, ringed by lamplight from the streets all around, the stretch of empty darkness. A cold wind blew suddenly, gustily, and the black shape of the plane tree rustled and then the sound was lost in the jet roar of an aeroplane going overhead.

I said, "It's like being in the country."

"Well, next best thing perhaps." She shivered. "Let's go in before we freeze." We stepped back through the glass door, and Maggie showed me the tiny kitchen which had been fashioned out of a deep cupboard, and then, halfway down the stairs, the bathroom, which we would all share. Finally, we ended up downstairs again in Maggie's warm, untidy sitting-room, and she found a bottle of sherry and some potato crisps which she swore were stale, but tasted all right to me. "Do you still want to come?" she asked.

"More than ever."

"When do you want to move in?"

"As soon as possible. Next week if I could."

"What about the girls you're sharing with just now?"

"They'll find someone else. One of them has a sister who's coming to London. I expect she'll move into my room."

"And what about furniture?"

"Oh . . . I'll manage."

"I expect," said Maggie comfortably, "your parents will come up trumps, they usually do. When I first came to London, my mother produced the most wonderful treasures out of the attic and the linen cupboard and so . . ." Her voice died away. I watched her in rueful silence, and she finally laughed at herself. "There I go again, opening my mouth and putting my foot in it. I'm sorry. I've obviously said something idiotically tactless."

"I haven't got a father, and my mother's abroad. She's living in Ibiza. That's really why I want somewhere of my own."

"I am sorry. I should have known, you spending Christmas with the Forbeses . . . I mean, I should have guessed."

"There's no reason why you should guess."

"Is your father dead?"

She was obviously curious, but in such an open and friendly way that all at once it seemed ridiculous to close up and shut up the way I usually did when people began asking me questions about my family.

"I don't think so," I said, trying to sound as though it didn't matter. "I think he lives in Los Angeles. He was an actor. My mother eloped with him when she was eighteen. But he soon got bored with domesticity, or perhaps he decided that his career was more important than raising a family. Anyway, the marriage lasted only a few months before he upped and left her, and then my mother had me."

"What a terrible thing to do."

"I suppose it was. I've never thought very much about it. My mother never talked about him. Not because she was particularly bitter or anything, just that when something was over and in the past, she usually forgot it. She's always been like that. She only looks forward, and always with the utmost optimism."

"But what happened after you were born? Did she go back to her parents?"

"No. Never."

"You mean, nobody sent a telegram saying 'Come back all is forgiven'?"

"I don't know. I honestly don't know."

"There must have been the most resounding row when your mother ran off, but even so . . ." Her voice trailed away. She was obviously unable to understand a situation which I had accepted with equanimity all my life. ". . . what sort of people would do a thing like that to their daughter?"

"I don't know."

"You must be joking!"

"No. I honestly don't know."

"You mean you don't know your own grandparents?"

"I don't even know who they are. Or perhaps who they were. I don't even know if they're still alive."

"Don't you know anything? Didn't your mother ever say anything?"

"Oh, of course . . . little scraps of the past used to come into her conversation but none of it added up to anything. You know how mothers talk to their children, remembering things that happened and things they used to do when they were little."

"But—Bayliss." She frowned. "That's not a very usual name. And it rings a bell somehow but I can't think why. Haven't you got a single clue?"

I laughed at her intensity. "You talk as though I really wanted to know. But you see, I don't. If you've never known grandparents, then you don't miss them."

"But don't you wonder . . ." she groped for words . . . "where they *lived?*"

"I know where they lived. They lived in Cornwall. In a stone house with fields that sloped down to the sea. And my mother had a brother called Roger but he was killed during the war."

"But what did she do after you were born? I suppose she had to go out and get a job."

"No, she had a little money of her own. A legacy from some old aunt or other. Of course, we never had a car or anything, but we seemed to manage all right. She had a flat in Kensington, in the basement of a house that belonged to some friends. And we stayed there till I was about eight, and then I went to boarding school, and after that we sort of . . . moved around . . ."

"Boarding schools cost money . . ."

"It wasn't a very grand boarding school."

"Did your mother marry again?"

I looked at Maggie. Her expression was lively and avidly curious, but she was kind. I decided that, having gone so far, I may as well tell her the rest.

"She . . . wasn't exactly the marrying type . . . But she was always very, very attractive, and I don't remember a time when there wasn't some adoring male in attendance . . . And once I was away at school, I suppose there wasn't much reason to go on being circumspect. I never knew where I was going to spend the next set of holidays. Once it was in France, in Provence. Sometimes in this country. Another time it was Christmas in New York."

Maggie took this in, and made a face. "Not much fun for you."

"But educational." I had long ago learned to make a joke of it. "And just think of all the places I've seen, and all the extraordinary places I've lived in. The Ritz in Paris once, and another time a gruesomely cold house in Denbighshire. That was a poet who thought he'd try sheep farming. I've never been so glad in my life when that association came to an end."

"She must be very beautiful."

"No, but men think she is. And she's very gay and improvident and vague, and I suppose you'd say utterly amoral. Maddening. Everything is 'jokey'. It's her big word. Unpaid bills are 'jokey' and lost handbags and unanswered letters, they're all 'jokey'. She has no idea of money and no sense of obligation. An embarrassing sort of person to live with."

"What's she doing in Ibiza?"

"She's living with some Swedish man she met out there. She went out to stay with a couple she knew, and she met this guy and the next thing I knew

I had a letter saying that she was going to move in with him. She said he was terribly Nordic and dour but he had a beautiful house."

"How long is it since you've seen her?"

"About two years. I eased out of her life when I was seventeen. I did a secretarial course and took temporary jobs, and finally I ended up working for Stephen Forbes."

"Do you like it?"

"Yes. I do."

"How old are you?"

"Twenty-one."

Maggie smiled again, shaking her long hair in wonderment. "What a lot you've done," she said, and she did not sound in the least bit sorry for me but even slightly envious. "At twenty-one I was a blushing bride in a beastly busty white wedding dress and an old veil that smelt of mothballs. I'm not really a trad. person, but I've got a mother who is, and I'm very fond of her so I usually used to do what she wanted."

I could imagine Maggie's mother. I said, resorting to the comfort of clichés, because I couldn't think of anything else to say, "Oh, well, it takes all sorts," and at that moment we heard John's key in the lock and after that we did not bring up the subject of mothers and families again.

It was a day like any other day, but it had a bonus attached to it. Last Thursday I had worked late with Stephen, trying to complete the last of the January

stocktaking, and in return he had given me this
morning off so that I had until lunchtime to my own
devices. I filled it in cleaning the flat (which took, at
most, no more than half an hour), doing some shopping and taking a bundle of clothes to the launder-
ette. By eleven thirty all this domesticity was completed so I put on my coat and set off, in a leisurely
way, for work, intending to walk some of the way,
and maybe stand myself an early lunch before getting
to the shop.

It was one of those cold, dark, damp days when
it never really gets light. I walked, through this
gloom, up into the New Kings Road, and headed
west. Here, every other shop seems to sell either antiques or second-hand beds or picture frames, and I
thought I knew them all, but all at once I found myself outside a shop which I had not noticed before.
The outside was painted white, the windows framed
in black, and there was a red and white awning
pulled out as protection against the imminent drizzle.

I looked up to see what the shop was called and
read the name TRISTRAM NOLAN picked out in neat
black Roman capitals over the door. This door was
flanked by windows filled with delectable odds and
ends and I paused to inspect their contents, standing
on the pavement bathed in brightness from the many
lights which burned within. Most of the furniture was
Victorian, re-upholstered and restored and polished.
A buttoned sofa with a wide lap and curly legs, a
sewing box, a small picture of lap dogs on a velvet
cushion.

I looked beyond the windows and into the shop itself, and it was then that I saw the cherrywood chairs. They were a pair, balloon backed, with curved legs and seats embroidered with roses.

I craved them. Just like that. I could picture them in my flat, and I wanted them desperately. For a moment I hesitated. This was no junk shop and the price might well be more than I could afford. But after all, no harm could be done by asking. Before I could lose my nerve, I opened the door and went in.

The shop was empty, but the door opening and closing had rung a bell, and presently there was the sound of someone coming down the stairs, the woollen curtain that hung over the door at the back of the shop was drawn aside and a man came into view.

I suppose I had expected someone elderly and formally attired, in keeping with the ambience of the shop and its contents, but this man's appearance rocked all my vague, preconceived notions. For he was young, tall and long-legged, dressed in jeans— faded to a soft blue and clinging like a second skin— and a blue denim jacket, equally old and faded, with the sleeves turned back in a businesslike way to reveal the checked cuffs of the shirt he wore beneath it. A cotton handkerchief was knotted at his neck and on his feet he wore soft moccasins, much decorated and fringed.

That winter the most unlikely people were drifting around London dressed as cowboys, but somehow this one looked real, and his worn clothes appeared as genuine as he was. We stood and looked at each other, and then he smiled and for some reason this took me unawares. I don't like being taken unawares, and I said "Good morning" with a certain coolness.

He dropped the curtain behind him and came forward, soft footed. "Can I help you?"

He may have looked like a genuine, dyed-in-the-wool American, but the moment he opened his mouth it was clear that he was no such thing. For some reason this annoyed me. The life I had led with my mother had left me with a thick streak of cynicism about men in general, and phoneys in particular, and this young man, I decided then and there, was a phoney.

"I . . . I was going to ask about these little chairs. The balloon-back ones."

"Oh, yes." He came forward to lay his hand on the back of one. The hand was long and shapely, with spade-tipped fingers, the skin very brown. "There's just the pair of them."

I stared at the chairs, trying to ignore his presence.

"I wondered how much they were."

He squatted beside me to search for a price ticket and I saw his hair fell thick and straight to his collar, very dark and lustrous.

"You're in luck," he told me. "They're going very cheap because the leg of one has been broken and then not very professionally repaired." He straightened up suddenly, surprising me by his height. His eyes were slightly tip-tilted, and a very dark brown, with an expression in them that I found disconcerting. He made me uncomfortable and my antipathy for him began to turn to dislike. "Fifteen pounds for the pair," he said. "But if you'd like to wait and pay a little more, I can get the leg reinforced, and perhaps a small veneer put over the joint. That would make it stronger and it would look better too."

"Isn't it all right now?"

"It would be all right for you," said the young man, ". . . but if you had a large fat man for dinner, he'd probably end up on his backside."

There was a pause while I regarded him—I hoped coldly. His eyes were brimming, with a malicious amusement which I had no intention of sharing. I did not appreciate the suggestion that the only men who would ever come and have dinner with me would necessarily be large and fat.

I said at last, "How much would it cost me to have the leg repaired?"

"Say five pounds. That means you get the chairs for a tenner each."

I worked this out, and decided that I could just afford them.

"I'll take them."

"Good," said the young man and put his fists on his hips and smiled amiably, as though this were the end of the transaction.

I decided he was utterly inefficient. "Do you want me to pay for them now, or to leave a deposit . . . ?"

"No, that doesn't matter. You can pay for them when you collect them."

"Well, when will they be ready?"

"In about a week."

"Don't you want my name?"

"Not unless you want to give it to me."

"What happens if I never come back?"

"Then I expect they'll be sold to someone else."

"I don't want to lose them."

"You won't," said the young man.

I frowned, angry with him, but he only smiled and went to the door to open it for me. Cold air poured in, and outside the drizzle had started and the street looked dark as night.

He said, "Goodbye," and I managed a frosty smile of thanks and went past him, out into the gloom, and as I did so I heard the bell ring as he shut the door behind me.

The day was, all at once, unspeakable. My pleasure in buying the chairs had been wrecked by the irritation which the young man had generated. I did not usually take instant dislikes to people and I was annoyed not only with him, but with myself, for being so vulnerable. I was still brooding on this when I walked down Walton Street and let myself into Stephen Forbes's bookshop. Even the comfort of being indoors and the pleasant smell of new paper and printers' ink did nothing to dispel my wretched mood.

The shop was on three levels, with new books on the ground floor, second-hand books and old prints upstairs, and Stephen's office in the basement. I saw that Jennifer, the second girl, was busy with a customer, and the only other person visible was an old lady in a tweed cape engrossed in the Gardening section, so I headed for the little cloakroom, unbuttoning my coat as I went, but then I heard Stephen's heavy, unmistakeable footsteps coming up from downstairs, and for some reason I stopped to wait for him. The next moment he appeared, tall, stooping and spectacled, with his usual expression of vague benevolence. He wore dark suits that always managed to appear as though in need of a good press, and already, at this early hour, the knot of his tie had begun to slip down, revealing the top button of his shirt.

"Rebecca," he said.

"Yes, I'm here . . ."

"I'm glad I've caught you." He came to my side speaking low-voiced, so as not to disturb the customers. "There's a letter for you downstairs; it's been forwarded on from your old flat. You'd better nip down and collect it."

I frowned. "A letter?"

"Yes. Airmail. Lots of foreign stamps. It has, for some reason, an air of urgency about it."

My irritation, along with all thoughts of new chairs, was lost in a sudden apprehension.

"Is it from my mother?"

"I don't know. Why don't you go and find out?"

So I went down the steep, uncarpeted stairs to the basement, lit, on this dark day, by long strip-lights let into the ceiling. The office was marvellously untidy—as usual—littered with letters and parcels and files, piles of old books, and cardboard boxes and ashtrays which nobody ever remembered to empty. But the letter was on the middle of Stephen's blotter and instantly visible.

I picked it up. An airmail envelope, Spanish stamps, an Ibizan postmark. But the writing was unfamiliar, pointed and spiky, as though a very fine pen had been used. It had been sent to the old flat, but this address had been crossed out and the address of the bookshop substituted in large, girlish, handwriting. I wondered how long the letter had lain on the table by the front door, before one of the girls realized that it was there and had taken the trouble to forward it on to me.

I sat down in Stephen's chair and slit the envelope. Inside, two pages of fine airmail paper, and the date at the head was the third of January. Very nearly a month ago. My mind sounded a note of alarm and, suddenly frightened, I began to read.

Dear Rebecca,

I hope you do not mind me calling you by your Christian name, but your mother has spoken to me of you a great deal. I am writing because your mother is very ill. She has been unwell for some time and I wished to write to you before but she would not let me.

Now, however, I am taking matters into my own hands, and with the doctor's approval I am

letting you know that I think you should come out
to see her.

If you can do this, perhaps you will cable me
the number of your aeroplane flight so that I can
be at the airport to meet you.

I know that you are working and it may not
be easy to make this trip, but I would advise you to
waste no time. I am afraid that you will find your
mother very changed, but her spirit is still high.

With good wishes.
Sincerely,
Otto Pedersen.

I sat in unbelief, and stared at the letter. The
formal words told me nothing and everything. My
mother was very ill, perhaps dying. A month ago I
had been asked to waste no time but to go to her.
Now it was a month later, and I had only just got the
letter and perhaps she was already dead—and I had
never gone. What would he think of me, this Otto
Pedersen whom I had never seen, whose name, even,
I had not known until this moment?

2

I read the letter again, and then again, the flimsy pages rustling in my hands. I was still there, sitting at his desk, when Stephen finally came downstairs to find me.

I turned to look up at him over my shoulder. He saw my face and said, "What is it?"

I tried to tell him, but could not. Instead I thrust the letter at him, and while he took it, and read it, I sat with my elbows on his desk, biting my thumbnails, bitter and angry, and fighting a terrible anxiety.

He was soon finished reading. He tossed the letter down on the desk between us, and said, "Did you know she was ill?"

I shook my head.

"When did you last hear from her?"

"Four, five months ago. She never wrote letters." I looked up at him and said, furiously, choked by the great lump in my throat, "That was nearly a *month* ago. That letter's been lying in the flat, and nobody bothered to send it to me. She may be dead by now and I never went, and she'll think I simply didn't care!"

"If she had died," said Stephen, "then we'd have surely heard. Now, don't cry, there isn't time for that. What we have to do is get you out to Ibiza with all convenient speed, and let—" he glanced down at the letter again—"Mr Pedersen know you're arriving. Nothing else matters."

I said, "I can't go," and my mouth began to grow square and my lower lip tremble as though I were a ten-year-old.

"Why can't you go?"

"Because I haven't got enough money for the fare."

"Oh, my dear child, let me worry about that . . ."

"But I can't let you . . ."

"Yes, you can, and if you get all stiff-necked about it then you can pay me back over the next five years and I'll charge you interest, if it'll make you feel happier, and now for God's sake don't let's mention it again . . ." He was already reaching for the directory, behaving in an altogether efficient and un-Stephen-like fashion. "Have you got a passport? And nobody's going to clamp down on you for smallpox injections or anything tiresome like that. Hallo? British Airways? I want to make a reservation on the first plane to Ibiza." He smiled down at me, still fighting tears and temper, but already feeling a little better. There is nothing like having a large and kindly man to take over in times of emotional stress. He picked up a pencil and drew a sheet of paper towards him and began to make notes. "Yes. When? Fine. Can we have a reservation, please? Miss Rebecca Bayliss. And what time does it get to Ibiza? And the flight number? Thank you so much. Thank you. Yes, I'll get her to the airport myself."

He put down the receiver and surveyed, with some satisfaction, the illegible squiggles his pencil had made.

"That's it, then. You fly tomorrow morning, change planes at Palma, get to Ibiza about half-past-seven. I'll drive you to the airport. No, don't start arguing again, I wouldn't feel happy unless I saw you actually walk on to the aeroplane. And now we'll cable Mr Otto Pedersen—" he picked up the letter again—"at the Villa Margareta, Santa Catarina, and let him know that you're coming." He smiled down at me with such cheerful reassurance that I was suddenly filled with hope.

I said, "I can't ever thank you . . ."

"I don't ever want you to," said Stephen. "It's the least I can do."

I flew the next day, in a plane half-filled with hopeful winter holiday tourists. They even carried straw hats against an improbably blazing sun, and their faces, as we stepped out into a steady drizzle at Palma, were disappointed but resolutely cheerful, as though, for certain, tomorrow would be better.

The rain never ceased, all the four hours I waited in the transit lounge, and the flight out of

Palma was bumpy with thick, wet clouds. But as we rose above them and headed out across the sea, the weather brightened. The clouds thinned and broke, disclosing an evening sky of robin's egg blue, and far below the crumpled sea was streaked with the pink light of the setting sun.

It was dark when we landed. Dark and damp. Coming down the gangway beneath a sky full of bright southern stars, there was only the smell of petrol, but as I walked across the puddled tarmac towards the lights of the terminal building I felt the soft wind in my face. It was warm and smelt of pines, and was evocative of every summer holiday I had ever spent abroad.

At this quiet time of the year the plane had not been full. It did not take long to get through Customs and Immigration, and—my passport stamped—I picked up my suitcase and walked into the Arrivals Lounge.

There were the usual small groups of waiting people standing about or sitting hunched apathetically on the long plastic banquettes. I stopped and looked about me, waiting to be identified, but could see nobody who looked in the least like a Swedish writer come to meet me. And then a man turned from buying a newspaper at the bookstall. Across the room our eyes met, and he folded the newspaper and began to walk towards me, pushing his paper into his jacket pocket as though it were no longer of any use to him. He was tall and thin, with hair that was either blond or white—it was impossible to tell in the bright, impersonal electric light. Before he was half way across the polished floor I smiled tentatively, and as he approached he said my name, "Rebecca?" with a question mark at the end of it, still not entirely certain that it was I.

"Yes."

"I'm Otto Pedersen." We shook hands and he gave a formal little bow as he did so. His hair, I saw then, was pale blond, turning grey, and his face was deeply tanned, thin and bony, the skin dry and finely wrinkled from long exposure to the sun. His eyes were very pale, and more grey than blue. He wore a black polo-necked sweater and a light oatmeal-coloured suit with pleated pockets, like a safari shirt, and a belt which hung loose, the buckle swinging. He smelt of aftershave and looked as clean as if he had been bleached.

Having found each other, it was suddenly difficult to find anything to say. All at once we were both overwhelmed by the circumstances of our meeting and I realized that he was as unsure of himself as I. But he was also urbane and polite, and dealt with this by taking my suitcase from me and asking if this was all my luggage.

"Yes, that's all."

"Then let us go to the car. If you like to wait at the door, I will fetch it and save you the walk . . ."

"I'll come with you."

"It's only across the road, in the car park."

So we went out together, into the darkness again. He led me to the half empty car park. Here, he stopped by a big black Mercedes, unlocked it, and tossed my case on to the back seat. Then he held the door open so that I could get in before coming around to the front of the car to settle himself beside me.

"I hope you had a good journey," he said, politely, as we left the terminal behind us and headed out into the road.

"It was a little bumpy in Palma. I had to wait four hours."

"Yes. There are no direct flights at this time of the year."

I swallowed. "I must explain about not answering your letter. I've moved flats, and I didn't get it till yesterday morning. It wasn't forwarded to me, you see. It was so good of you to write, and you must have wondered why I never replied."

"I thought something like that must have happened."

His English was perfect, only the precise Swedish vowel sounds betraying his origins, and a certain formality in the manner in which he expressed himself.

"When I got your letter I was so frightened . . . that it would be too late."

"No," said Otto. "It is not too late."

Something in his voice made me look at him. His profile was knife sharp against the yellow glow of passing street lights, his expression unsmiling and grave.

I said, "Is she dying?"

"Yes," said Otto. "Yes, she is dying."

"What is wrong with her?"

"Cancer of the blood. You call it leukaemia."

"How long has she been ill?"

"About a year. But it was only just before Christmas time that she became so ill. The doctor thought that we should try blood transfusions, and I took her to the hospital for this. But it was no good, because as soon as I got her home again, she started this very bad nose bleed, and so the ambulance had to come and take her back to hospital again. She was there over Christmas and only then allowed home again. It was after that I wrote to you."

"I wish I'd got the letter in time. Does she know I'm coming?"

"No, I didn't tell her. You well know how she loves surprises, and equally how she hates to be disappointed. I thought there was a chance that something would go wrong and you wouldn't be on the plane." He smiled frostily, "But of course you were."

We stopped at a cross-roads to wait for a country cart to pass in front of us, the feet of the mule making a pleasant sound on the dusty road, and a lantern swinging from the back of the cart. Otto took advantage of the pause to take a cheroot from the breast pocket of his jacket and light it from the lighter on the dashboard. The cart passed, we moved on.

"How long is it since you have seen your mother?"

"Two years."

"You must expect a great change. I am afraid

you will be shocked, but you must try not to let her see. She is still very vain."

"You know her so well."

"But of course."

I longed to ask him if he loved her. The question was on the tip of my tongue, but I realized that at this stage of our acquaintance it would be nothing but impertinence to ask such an intimate and personal thing. Besides, what difference did it make? He had met her and wanted to be with her, had given her a home, and now, when she was so ill, was cherishing her in his own apparently unemotional manner. If that wasn't love, then what was?

After a little, we began to talk of other things. I asked him how long he had lived on the island, and he said five years. He had come first in a yacht and had liked the place so well that he had returned the next year to buy his house and settle here.

"You're a writer . . ."

"Yes, but I am also a Professor of History."

"Do you write books on history?"

"I have done so. At the moment I am working on a thesis concerned with the Moorish occupation of these islands and southern Spain."

I was impressed. As far as I could remember, none of my mother's previous lovers had been even remotely intellectual.

"How far away is your house?"

"About five miles now. The village of Santa Catarina was quite unspoiled when I first came here. Now, however, large hotel developments are planned and I fear it will become spoiled like the rest of the island. No, that is wrong. Like some parts of the island. It is still possible to be entirely remote if you know where to go and have a car or perhaps a motor boat."

It was warm in the car and I rolled down the window. The soft night air blew in on my face and I saw that we were in country now, passing through groves of olives, with every now and then the glimmering light of a farmhouse window shining beyond the bulbous, spiked shapes of prickly pear.

I said, "I'm glad she was here. I mean, if she has to be ill and die, I'm glad it's somewhere like this, in the south, with the sun warm and the smell of pines."

"Yes," said Otto. And then, precisely as ever, "I think that she has been very happy."

We drove on in silence, the road empty, telegraph poles rushing to meet the headlights of the car. I saw that now we were running parallel to the sea, which spread to an invisible, dark horizon and was dotted here and there with the lights of fishing boats. Presently there appeared ahead of us the neon-lighted shape of a village. We passed a sign reading "Santa Catarina" and then were driving down the main street; the air was filled with the smell of onions and oil and grilling meat. Flamenco music flung itself at us from open doorways, and dark faces, filled with absent curiosity, turned to watch us pass. In a moment we had left the village behind us, and had plunged forward into the darkness which lay beyond, only to slow down almost immediately to negotiate a steep corner which led up a narrow lane between orchards of almond trees. The headlights bored into the darkness, and ahead I saw the villa, white and square, pierced by small, secretive windows and with a lighted lantern swinging over the great, nailed front door.

Otto braked the car and switched off the engine. We got out, Otto taking my suitcase from the back seat and leading the way across the gravel. He opened the door and stood aside and I walked in ahead of him.

We were in a hallway, lit by a wrought-iron chandelier and furnished with a long couch covered in a bright blanket. A tall blue and white jar stood by the door containing a selection of ivory-handled walking sticks and sun umbrellas. As Otto closed the front door, another opened ahead of us and a small, dark-haired woman appeared, wearing a pink overall and flat, worn slippers.

"Señor."

"Maria."

She smiled, showing a number of gold teeth. He spoke to her in Spanish, asking a question to which she replied and then, turning, introduced me to her.

"This is Maria, who takes care of us. I have told her who you are . . ."

I held out my hand and Maria took it: we made friends by smiling and nodding. Then she turned back to Otto and spoke some more. Presently he handed her my suitcase, and she withdrew.

Otto said, "Your mother has been asleep but she is awake now. Let me take your coat."

I unbuttoned it, and he helped me off with it and laid it across the end of the couch. Then he went across the floor towards yet another door, motioning me to follow. I did, and was suddenly nervous, afraid of what I was going to find.

It was the salon of the house into which he led me. A long low-ceilinged room, white-washed like the rest of the house, and furnished with a pleasing mixture of modern Scandinavian and antique Spanish. The tile floor was scattered with rugs, there were a great many books and pictures, and in the centre of the room a round table was laid out, seductively, with neatly ordered magazines and newspapers.

A wood fire burned in a great stone fireplace, and in front of this was a bed, with a low table alongside, holding a glass of water and a jug, a few pink geraniums in a mug, some books and a lighted lamp.

This lamp and the flicker of flames provided the only light in the room, but from the door I could see the narrow shape which humped the pink blankets and the attenuated hand and arm which was extended as Otto came forward to stand on the hearth rug.

"Darling," she said.

"Lisa." He took the hand and kissed it.

"You haven't been long after all."

"Maria says you have slept. Do you feel ready for a visitor?"

"A visitor?" Her voice was a thread. "Who?"

Otto glanced up at me, and I moved forward to stand beside him. I said, "It's me. Rebecca."

"Rebecca. Darling child. Oh, how blissfully jokey." She held out both arms to me, and I knelt down beside the bed to kiss her; her body gave me no resistance or support at all, so thin was she, and when I touched her cheek it felt papery beneath my lips. It was like kissing a leaf that has long since been wrenched by the wind from its parent tree.

"But what are you doing *here?*" She looked over my shoulder at Otto, and then back at me again. She put on the pretence of a frown. "You didn't *tell* her to come?"

"I thought you would like to see her," said Otto. "I thought it would cheer you up."

"But darling, why didn't you tell me?"

I smiled. "We wanted it to be a surprise."

"But I wish I'd known, then I could have looked forward to seeing you. That's what we always used to think, before Christmas. Half the fun was anticipation." She let me go and I sat back on my heels. "Are you going to stay?"

"For a day or so."

"Oh, how utterly perfect. We can have the most gorgeous gossips. Otto, does Maria know she's staying?"

"Of course."

"And what about dinner tonight?"

"It's all arranged . . . we'll have it together, in here, just the three of us."

"Well, let's have something now. A little drinkey. Is there any champagne?"

Otto smiled. "I think I can find a bottle. In fact, I think I remembered to put one on ice for just such an occasion."

"Oh, you clever man."

"Shall I get it now?"

"Please, darling."

She slid her hand in mine and it was like holding chicken bones. "And we'll drink to being together."

He went away to fetch the champagne and we were alone. I found a little stool and pulled it up so that I could sit close to her. We looked at each other, and she could not stop smiling. The dazzling smile and the bright dark eyes were still the same, so was the dark hair that spread like a stain over the snowy pillowcase. Otherwise her appearance was horrifying. I had never known anyone could be so thin and still be alive. And to make it more unreal, she was not pale and colourless but quite brown, as though she still spent most of the day lying in the sun. But she was excited. It seemed she could not stop talking.

"So sweet of the darling man to know how much I would love to see you. The only thing is, I'm so boring just now, I don't feel like doing anything, he should have waited until I'm better and then we could have had some fun together, and gone swimming and out in the boat and had picnics and things."

I said, "I can come again."

"Yes, of course you can." She touched my face

with her hand as though needing this contact to reassure her that I was really there. "You're looking gorgeous, do you know that? You've got your father's colouring, with those big grey eyes, and that corn-coloured hair. Is it corn, or is it gold? And I love the way you're doing it." Her hand travelled to the single plait which fell forward, like a rope over my right shoulder. "It makes you look like something out of a fairy story; you know, those old-fashioned books with the magical pictures. You're very pretty."

I shook my head. "No. I'm not."

"Well, you look it, and that's the next best thing. Darling, what are you doing with yourself? It's such ages since I wrote or heard from you. Whose fault was that. Mine, I suppose, I'm hopeless at writing letters."

I told her about the book shop and the new flat. She was amused by this. "What a funny person you are, building a little nest for yourself without anybody to share it with. Haven't you met anybody yet you want to marry?"

"No. Nor anyone who wants to marry me."

She looked malicious. "What about the man you work for?"

"He's married, he's got a charming wife and a brood of children."

She giggled. "That never bothered me. Oh, darling, what a dreadful mother I was to you, trailing you round in that reprehensible fashion. It's a wonder you haven't collected the most ghastly selection of neuroses or hang-ups or whatever they call them

these days! But you don't look as though you have, so
perhaps it was all right after all."

"Of course it was all right. I just grew up with
my eyes open and that was no bad thing." I added, "I
like Otto."

"Isn't he divine? So correct and punctilious and
northern. And so blazingly intelligent . . . So lucky
he doesn't want me to be intelligent too! He just likes
having me make him laugh."

Somewhere, in the middle of the house, a clock
struck seven, and as the last note chimed Otto came
back into the room carrying a tray with the champagne bottle in a bucket of ice, and three wine glasses.
We watched as he expertly loosened the cork and the
golden foaming wine spilled into the three glasses,
and we each took one and raised them, all of us smiling because it was suddenly a party. My mother said,
"Here's to the three of us and happy times. Oh, so
divinely jokey."

Later, I was shown to my bedroom, which was
either simply luxurious or luxuriously simple, I
couldn't decide which. A fitted bathroom led off it, so
I showered, and changed into trousers and a silk
shirt, and brushed my hair and replaited it, and returned to the salon. I found Otto and my mother
waiting for me, Otto also changed for the evening,
and Mother wearing a fresh bedjacket of powder blue
with a silk shawl embroidered with pink roses flung
across her knees, its long fringe brushing the floor.
We had another drink and then Maria served dinner
on a low table by the fire. My mother never stopped

talking—it was all about the old days when I was growing up, and I kept thinking that Otto would be shocked, but he wasn't shocked at all, he was curious and much amused and kept asking questions and prompting my mother to tell us more.

". . . and that dreadful farm in Denbighshire . . . Rebecca, do you remember that terrible house? We nearly died of cold and the fire smoked whenever we lit it. That was Sebastian," she explained for Otto's benefit. "We all thought he was going to be a famous poet, but he wasn't any better at writing poetry than he was at sheep farming. In fact, if anything, worse. And I couldn't think how on earth I could leave him without hurting his feelings and then luckily Rebecca got bronchitis so I had the most perfect excuse."

"Not so lucky for Rebecca," suggested Otto.

"It certainly was. She hated it just as much as I did; anyway he had a horrible dog that was always threatening to bite her. Darling, is there any more champagne?"

She ate hardly anything, but sipped glass after glass of the icy wine while Otto and I worked our way steadily through Maria's delicious, four-course dinner. When it was finished, and the dishes cleared away, my mother asked for some music, and Otto put a Brahms concerto on the record player, turned very low. Mother just went on talking, like a toy that has been overwound and will only stop whirring senselessly around the floor when it finally breaks.

Presently, saying that he had work to do, Otto

excused himself and left us, first building up the fire with fresh logs and making sure that we had everything we needed.

"Does he work every evening?" I asked, when he had gone.

"Nearly always. And in the mornings. He's very punctilious. I think that's why we've got on so well because we're so different."

I said, "He adores you."

"Yes," said my mother, accepting this. "And the best bit is that he never tried to turn me into someone else; he just accepted me, with my wicked ways and my lurid past." She touched my plait again. "You're growing more like your father . . . I always thought you looked like me, but you don't, you look like him now. He was very handsome."

"You know, I don't even know what his name was."

"Sam Bellamy. But Bayliss is a much better name, don't you think? Besides, having you all on my own like that, I always felt you were my child and nobody else's."

"I wish you'd tell me about him. You never have."

"There's so little to tell. He was an actor, and too good-looking for words."

"But where did you meet him?"

"He came down to Cornwall with a Summer Stock company doing open-air Shakespeare. It was all terribly romantic, dark blue summer nights and

the damp, dewy smell of the grass, and that divine
Mendelssohn music and Sam being Oberon.

> Through the house give glimmering light,
> By the dead and drowsy fire;
> Every elf and fairy sprite;
> Hop as light as bird from brier.

It was magical. And falling in love with him was part
of the magic."

"Was he in love with you?"

"We both thought he was."

"But you ran away with him, and married
him . . ."

"Yes. But only because my parents left me with
no alternative."

"I don't understand."

"They disliked him. They disapproved. They
said I was too young. My mother said why didn't I
marry some nice young man who lived locally, why
didn't I settle down and stop making an exhibition of
myself? And if I married an actor, what would people say? I sometimes thought that was all she cared
about, what people would say. As if it could possibly
matter what anybody said."

It was, unbelievably, the first time I had ever
heard her mention her mother. I said, cautiously
prompting, "Didn't you like her?"

"Oh, darling, it's so long ago. It's so difficult to
remember. But she stifled and repressed me. I sometimes felt she was trying to choke me with conven-

tions. And Roger had been killed and I missed him so
dreadfully. Everything would have been different if
Roger had been there." She smiled. "He was so nice.
Almost too nice. A real BV right from the very
start."

"What's a BV?"

"Bitches' Victim. He always fell in love with the
most impossible girls. And finally he married one. A
little blonde doll, with dolly hair and dolly china blue
eyes. My mother thought she was sweet. I couldn't
stand her."

"What was she called?"

"Mollie." She made a face as though the very
word tasted bad.

I laughed. "She can't have been as bad as all
that."

"I thought she was. So maddeningly tidy. Always cleaning out her handbag or putting her shoes
into trees, or sterilizing the baby's toys."

"She had a baby then?"

"Yes, a little boy. Poor child, she insisted on
calling him Eliot."

"I think that's a nice name."

"Oh, Rebecca, it's sickening." It was obvious
that nothing Mollie had done could find favour in my
mother's eyes. "I always felt sorry for the child, being
saddled with such a dreadful name. And somehow he
lived up to it, you know how people do, and after
Roger was killed the poor scrap was worse than ever,
always hanging round his mother's neck and having
to have a light on in his room at night."

"I think you're being very unkind."

She laughed. "Yes, I know, and it wasn't his fault. He probably turned into quite a personable young man if his mother gave him half a chance."

"I wonder what happened to Mollie?"

"I don't know. I don't particularly care, either." My mother could always be cruelly off-hand. "It's like a dream. Like remembering dream people. Or perhaps—" her voice trailed away—"perhaps they were real and I was the dream."

I felt uncomfortable, because this was too near the truth that I was trying to keep at bay. I said quickly, "Are your parents still alive?"

"My mother died that Christmas we spent in New York. Do you remember that Christmas? The cold and the snow and all the shops full of the sound of 'Jingle Bells'? By the end of that Christmas I felt I never wanted to hear that damned tune again. My father wrote to me, but of course the letter didn't reach me until months later by which time it had followed me half round the world. And then it was really too late to write and say anything. Besides, I'm so useless about writing letters. He probably thought I simply didn't care."

"Didn't you ever write?"

"No."

"Didn't you like him either?" It seemed a sorry state of affairs.

"Oh, I adored him. He was wonderful. Terribly good looking, attractive to women, frightfully fierce and frightening. He was a painter. Did I ever tell you that?"

A painter. I had imagined everything, but never a painter. "No, you never said."

"Well, if you'd had any sort of education at all you'd probably have guessed. Grenville Bayliss. Doesn't that mean anything to you at all?"

I shook my head sadly. It was terrible never to have heard of a famous grandfather.

"Well, why should it? I was never any good at trailing you round art galleries or museums. come to think of it, I was never much good at anything. It's a wonder you've turned out so well on a solid diet of maternal neglect."

"What did he look like?"

'Who?"

"Your father."

"How do you imagine him?"

I considered the question and came up with Augustus John. "Bohemian, and bearded and rather leonine . . ."

"Wrong," said my mother. "He wasn't like that at all. He started off his life in the Navy and the Navy left an indelible stamp on him. You see, he didn't decide to be a painter until he was nearly thirty, when he threw up a promising career and enrolled at the Slade. It nearly broke my mother's heart. And moving to Cornwall and setting up house at Porthkerris simply added insult to injury. I don't think she ever forgave him for being so selfish. She'd adored queening it in Malta, and probably fancied herself as wife to the Commander-in-Chief. I must say, he was tailor-made for the part, very blue-eyed and imposing and terrifying. He never lost what was known in those days as a quarter-deck manner."

"But you weren't terrified of him?"

"No. I loved him."

"Then why didn't you go home?"

Her face closed up. "I couldn't. I wouldn't. Terrible things had been said, by all of us. Old resentments and old truths had all come boiling up, and threats were made and ultimatums handed out. And the more they opposed me, the more determined I became, and the more impossible it was, when the time came, to admit that they'd been right, and I'd been wrong, and I'd made a hideous mistake. And if I had gone home, I would never have got away again. I knew that. And you wouldn't have belonged to me any more, you'd have belonged to your grandmother. I couldn't have borne that. You were such a precious little thing." She smiled and added rather wistfully, "And we did have fun, didn't we?"

"Yes, of course we did."

"I would have liked to go back. Sometimes I very nearly did. It was such a lovely house. Boscarva it was called, and it was rather like this villa, standing square on a hill above the sea. When Otto first brought me here, it reminded me of Boscarva. But here it's warm and the winds are gentle; there, it was wild and stormy, and the garden was honeycombed with tall hedges to shelter the flower beds from the sea winds. I think the wind was the thing that my mother most hated. She used to seal all the windows and shut herself indoors, playing bridge with her friends or doing needlepoint."

"Didn't she ever do things with you?"

"Not really."

"But who looked after you?"

"Pettifer. And Mrs Pettifer."

"Who were they?"

"Pettifer had been in the Navy, too; he looked after my father and cleaned the silver and sometimes drove the car. And Mrs Pettifer did the cooking. I can't tell you how cosy they were. Sitting by the kitchen fire with them making toast and listening to the wind battering at the windows, knowing that it couldn't get in . . . it made you feel so safe. And we used to read fortunes from the teacups . . ." Her voice trailed off, memories uncertain now. And then, "No, that was Sophia."

"Who was Sophia?"

She did not reply. She was staring at the fire, her expression far away. Perhaps she had not heard me. She said at last, "After my mother died I should have gone back. It was naughty of me to stay away, but I was never over-endowed with what is known as moral fibre. But, you know, there are things at Boscarva that belong to me."

"What sort of things?"

"A desk, I remember. A little one, with drawers down the side, and a lid that opened up. I think it's called a davenport. And some jade that my father brought home from China and a Venetian looking-glass. They were all mine. On the other hand, I moved around so much that they would just have been a nuisance." She looked at me, frowning a little. "But perhaps you don't think they are a nuisance. Have you got any furniture in this flat of yours?"

"No. Practically none."

"Then perhaps I'll see if I can get hold of them for you. They must still be at Boscarva, provided the house hasn't been sold or burned down or something. Would you like me to try and get hold of them?"

"More than anything. Not just because I need furniture, but because they belonged to you."

"Oh, darling, how sweet, too jokey the way you long for roots, and I could never bear to have any. I always felt they would just tie me down in one place."

"And I always feel that they would make me belong."

She said, "You belong to me."

We stayed talking until the early hours of the morning. About midnight, she asked me to refill her waterjug, and I found my way into the deserted kitchen and did this for her, and realized then that Otto, with gentle tact, had probably taken himself quietly off to bed, so that we could be together. And when at last her voice grew tired and her words began to trail off in a blur of exhaustion, I said that I was sleepy too, which I was, and I stood up, cramped from sitting, stretched, and put more logs on the fire. Then I took away her second pillow so that she lay, ready for sleep. The silken shawl had slipped to the floor, so I picked this up and folded it and laid it on a chair. It remained only to stoop and kiss her, turn off the lamp, and leave her there in the firelight. As I went through the door, she said, as she always used to say when I was a little girl, "Good night, my love. Goodbye until tomorrow."

The next morning I was awake early, aware of sunshine streaming through the gaps in the shutters. I got up and went to open them, and saw the brilliant Mediterranean morning. I stepped out through the open windows on to the stone terrace which ran the length of the house and saw the hill sloping down to the sea, maybe a mile distant. The sand-coloured land was veiled in pink, the first tender blossoms of the almond trees. I went back into my room, dressed, and went out again—across the terrace, down a flight of steps, and through the ordered, formal garden. I vaulted a low stone wall, and walked on in the direction of the sea. Presently, I found myself in an orchard, surrounded by almond trees. I stopped and looked up at a froth of pink blossom and beyond it a pale and cloudless blue sky.

I knew that each flower would bear a precious fruit which, when the time came, would be frugally cropped, but even so I could not resist picking a single spray, and I was still carrying this when an hour or so later, having walked to the sea and back, I retraced my steps up the hill towards the villa.

It was steeper than I had realized. Pausing for breath, I looked up at the house, and saw Otto Pedersen standing on the terrace watching my progress. For an instant we both stood still; then he moved and started down the steps, and came down the garden to meet me.

I went on more slowly, still holding the spray of blossom. I knew then. I knew before he came close enough for me to see the expression on his face, but I went on, up through the orchard, and we met at last by the little drystone wall.

He said my name. That was all.

I said, "I know. You don't have to tell me."

"She died during the night. When Maria went in this morning to wake her . . . it was all over. It was so peaceful."

It occurred to me that we were not doing much to comfort each other. Or maybe there was no need. He put out a hand to help me over the wall, and kept my hand in his as we walked together up through the garden to the house.

She was buried, according to Spanish law, that very day, and in the little churchyard in the village. There was only the priest present, and Otto and Maria and myself. When it was all over, I put the spray of almond blossom on to her grave.

I flew back to London the next morning, and Otto drove me to the airport in his car. For most of the time we travelled in silence, but as we approached the terminal he suddenly said, "Rebecca, I don't know whether this has any significance, but I would have married Lisa. I would have married her, but I already

have a wife in Sweden. We do not live together, and
have not done so for a number of years, but she will
not divorce me because her religion will not allow it."

"You didn't need to tell me, Otto."

"I wanted you to know."

"You made her so happy. You took such care of
her."

"I am glad that you came. I am glad that you
saw her."

"Yes." There was, all at once, a terrible lump in
my throat, and my eyes filled and brimmed with
painful tears. "Yes, I am glad too."

In the terminal, my ticket and my luggage
checked, we stood and faced each other.

"Don't wait," I said. "Go now. I hate good-
byes."

"All right . . . but first . . ." He felt in his
jacket pocket and took out three fine, worn silver
bracelets. My mother had worn them always. She
had been wearing them that last night. "You must
have these." He took my hand and slipped them on
to my wrist. "And this." Out of another pocket came
a folded wad of British notes. He pressed it into my
palm and closed my fingers over it. "They were in her
handbag . . . so you must have them."

I knew they hadn't been in her handbag. She had
never any money in her handbag except a few cop-
pers for the next telephone call, and some dog-eared
bills, long overdue. But there was something in Otto's
face that I couldn't refuse, so I took the money and

kissed him, and he turned on his heel, without a word.

I flew back to London in a state of miserable indecision. Emotionally I was empty, drained even of grief. Physically I found that I was exhausted but I could neither sleep nor face the meal that the stewardess offered me. She brought me tea and I tried to drink that, but it tasted bitter and I left it to grow cold.

It was as though a long-locked door had been opened, but only a crack, and it was up to me to open it wide, although what lay behind it was dark and fraught with uncertainty.

Perhaps I should go to Cornwall and seek out my mother's family, but the glimpses I had been given of the set-up at Porthkerris were not encouraging. My grandfather would be very old, lonely and probably bitter. I realized that I had made no arrangement with Otto Pedersen about letting him know that my mother was dead, and so there was the hideous possibility that if I went to see him, I should be the one who would have to break the news. As well, I blamed him a little for having let his daughter make such a mess of her life. I knew that she was impulsive and thoughtless, and stubborn too, but surely he could have been a little more positive in his dealings with her. He could have sought her out, offered to help, inspected me, his grandchild. But he had done none of these things, and surely this would always stand like a high wall between us.

And yet, I longed for roots. I did not necessarily

want to live with them, but I wanted them to be
there. There were things at Boscarva that had belonged to my mother, and so now belonged to me.
She had wanted me to have them, had said as much,
so perhaps I was under an obligation to go to Cornwall and claim them as my own, but to go only for
this reason seemed both soulless and greedy.

I leaned back and dozed and heard again my
mother's voice.

*I was never frightened of him. I loved him. I
should have gone back.*

And she had said a name—Sophia—but I had
never found out who Sophia was.

I slept at last and dreamed that I was there. But
the house in my dream had no shape or form and the
only real thing about it was the sound of the wind,
battering its way inland, fresh and cold from the open
sea.

I was in London by the early afternoon, but the dark
day had lost its shape and meaning, and I could not
think what I was meant to do with what remained of
it. In the end I got a taxi and went to Walton Street to
seek out Stephen Forbes.

I found him upstairs, going through a box of
books out of an old house which had just been sold
up. There was no one else with him, and as I appeared at the top of the stairs he stood up and came
towards me, thinking that I was a potential customer.
When he saw that I was not, his manner changed.

"Rebecca! You're back."

I stood there, with my hands in my coat pockets.

"Yes. I got in about two." He watched me, his face a question. I said, "My mother died, early yesterday morning. I was just in time. I had an evening with her, and we talked and talked."

"I see," said Stephen. "I'm glad you saw her." He cleared some books from the edge of a table, and leaned against it, folding his arms and eyeing me through his spectacles. He said, "What are you going to do now?"

"I don't know."

"You look exhausted. Why not take a few days off?"

I said again, "I don't know."

He frowned. "What don't you know?"

"I don't know what to do."

"What's the problem?"

"Stephen, have you ever heard of an artist called Grenville Bayliss?"

"Heavens, yes. Why?"

"He's my grandfather."

Stephen's face was a study. "Good Lord. When did you find that out?"

"My mother told me. I'd never heard of him," I had to admit.

"You should have."

"Is he well known?"

"He was, twenty years ago when I was a boy. There was a Grenville Bayliss over the dining-room fireplace in my father's old house in Oxford. Part of my growing up, one might say. A grey stormy sea and a fishing boat with a brown sail. Used to make me feel seasick to look at it. He specialized in seascapes."

"He was a sailor. I mean, he'd been in the Royal Navy."

"That follows."

I waited for him to go on, but he was silent. I said at last, "What am I to do, Stephen?"

"What do you want to do, Rebecca?"

"I never had a family."

"Is it so important?"

"Suddenly it is."

"Then go and see him. Is there any reason not to?"

"I'm frightened."

"Of what?"

"I don't know. Of being snubbed, I suppose. Or ignored."

"Were there dreadful family rows?"

"Yes. And cuttings off. And never darken my door again. You know the sort of thing."

"Did your mother suggest that you went?"

"No. Not in so many words. But she said there were some things that belonged to her. She thought I should have them."

"What sort of things?"

I told him. "I know it's nothing very much. Perhaps not even worth making the journey for. But I'd like to have something that belonged to her. Besides —" I tried to turn it into a joke—"they might help to fill up some of the blank spaces in the new flat."

"I think collecting your possessions should be a secondary reason for going to Cornwall. Your first should be making friends with Grenville Bayliss."

"Supposing he doesn't want to make friends?"

"Then no harm has been done. Except possibly a little bruising to your pride, but that won't kill you."

"You're rail-roading me into this," I told him.

"If you didn't want my advice, then why did you come to see me?"

He had a point. "I don't know," I admitted.

He laughed. "You don't know much, do you?" and when at last I smiled back, he said, "Look. Today's Thursday. Go home and get some sleep. And if tomorrow's too soon, then go down to Cornwall on Sunday or Monday. Just go. See how the land lies, see how the old boy is. It may take a few days, but that doesn't matter. Don't come back to London until you've done all you can. And if you can get hold of your own bits and pieces, well and good, but remember that they're of secondary importance."

"Yes. I'll remember."

He stood up. "Then push off," he said. "I've got enough to do without wasting my time running a private Tell Auntie column on your account."

"Can I come back to work when all this is over?"

"You better had. I can't manage without you."

"Goodbye then," I said.

"Au revoir," said Stephen, and as if on an afterthought, leaned forward to give me a clumsy kiss. "And Good Luck!"

I had already spent enough money on taxis, so, still carrying my case, I walked up to the bus stop and waited until one came, and lurched my way back to Fulham. Gazing, unseeing, out of the window at the grey, crowded streets, I tried to make some plans. I would go to Cornwall, as Stephen suggested, on Monday. At this time of year it shouldn't be difficult to get a seat on the train or find somewhere to stay when I finally got to Porthkerris. And Maggie would keep an eye on my flat.

Thinking of the flat made me remember the chairs I had bought before I had gone to Ibiza. That day seemed a lifetime ago. But if I did not claim them then they would be sold as the disagreeable young man had threatened. With this in mind, I got off the bus a few stops before my own so that I could call into the shop and pay for the chairs and thus be certain that they would be waiting for me when I returned.

I had steeled myself to do business once more with the young man in the blue denims, but as I let myself in and the bell rang with the opening and the closing of the door, I saw with some relief that it was not he who stood up from behind the desk at the back of the shop, but another man, older, with grey hair and a dark beard.

He came forward, taking off a pair of horn-rimmed spectacles, as I thankfully put down my suitcase.

"Good afternoon."

"Oh, good afternoon. I came about some chairs

I bought last Monday. Cherrywood, balloon-back ones."

"Oh, yes, I know."

"One of them had to be repaired."

"It's been done. Do you want to take them with you?"

"No. I've got a suitcase. I can't carry them. And I'm going away for a few days. But I thought if I paid for them now, perhaps you'd keep them until I got back."

"Yes, of course." He had a charming, deep voice, and when he smiled his rather saturnine face lit up.

I began to open my bag. "Will it be all right if I write you a cheque? I've got a Bankers Card."

"That's all right . . . would you like to use my desk? And here's a pen."

I began to write. "Who shall I make it out to?"

"To me. Tristram Nolan."

I was gratified to know that it was he who owned this pleasant shop and not my mannerless, cowboy friend. I wrote the cheque and crossed it, and handed it to him. He stood, head down, reading it, and took so long that I thought I must have forgotten something.

"Have I put the date?"

"Yes, that's perfect." He looked up. "It's just your name. Bayliss. It's not very common."

"No. No it's not."

"Are you any relation to Grenville Bayliss?"

Having his name flung at me, just now, was extraordinary and yet not extraordinary at all, in the same way that a name, or a relevant item of news, will spring at you, unbidden, from a page of close print.

I said, "Yes, I am." And then because there was no reason why he shouldn't know, "He's my grandfather."

"Extraordinary," he said.

I was puzzled. "Why?"

"I'll show you." He laid my cheque down on his desk and went to pull out from behind a drop-leafed sofa table a large, sturdy oil painting in a gilt frame. He held it up, balancing one corner on his desk, and I saw that it was by my grandfather. His signature was in the corner, and the date below it, 1932.

"I've only just bought it. It needs cleaning, of course, but I think it's very charming."

I stepped closer to inspect it, and saw sand dunes in an evening light, and two young boys, naked, bent over a collection of shells. The work was perhaps old-fashioned, but the composition charming —the colouring delicate and yet somehow robust—as though the boys, vulnerable in their nakedness, were still tough, and creatures to be reckoned with.

"He was good, wasn't he?" I said, and could not hide the note of pride in my voice.

"Yes. A marvellous colourist." He put the picture back. "Do you know him well?"

"I don't know him at all. I've never met him."

He said nothing, simply stood, waiting for me to enlarge on this odd statement. To fill the silence I went on. "But I've decided that perhaps it's time I did. In fact, I'm going to Cornwall on Monday."

"But that's splendid. The roads will be empty at this time of the year, and it's a lovely drive."

"I'm going by train. I haven't got a car."

"It will still be a pleasant journey. I hope the sun shines for you."

"Thank you very much."

We moved back to the door. He opened it, I picked up my suitcase. "You'll look after my chairs for me?"

"Of course. Goodbye. And have a good time in Cornwall."

3

But the sun did not shine for me. Monday dawned grey and depressing as ever and my faint hopes that the weather would improve as the train rocketed westwards soon died, for the sky darkened with every mile and the wind got up and the day finally dissolved into pouring rain. There was nothing to be seen from the streaming windows; only the blurred shapes of hills and farmsteads, and every now and then the clustered roofs of a village flashed by, or we raced through the half-empty station of some small anonymous town.

By Plymouth, I comforted myself, it would be different. We would cross the Saltash Bridge and find ourselves in another country, another climate, where there would be pink-washed cottages and palm trees and thin winter sunshine. But of course all that happened was that the rain fell even more relentlessly; as I stared out at flooded fields and leafless wind-torn trees, my hopes finally died and I began to be discouraged.

It was nearly a quarter to five by the time we

reached the junction which was the end of my journey, and the dark afternoon had sunk, already, into twilight. As the train slowed down alongside the platform, I saw an incongruous palm tree, silhouetted like a broken umbrella against the streaming sky, and the falling rain shimmered and danced in front of the lighted sign which said "St Abbotts, change for Porthkerris." The train finally stopped. I shouldered my rucksack and opened the heavy door which was instantly torn out of my grasp by the wind. The sudden impact of strong cold air, driven inland, over the dark sea, made me gasp, and with some idea of making haste I picked up my bag and jumped out on to the platform. I followed the general exodus of travellers up and over the wooden bridge to the station building on the far side. Most of the other passengers seemed to have friends to meet them, or else walked through the ticket office in a purposeful fashion, as though knowing that a car was waiting for them on the far side. Blindly, I followed them, feeling very new and strange but hoping that they would lead me to a taxi. But when I came out into the station yard, there were no taxis. I stood about, hopeful of being offered a lift, but too shy to ask for one, until the tail light of the last car, inevitably, disappeared up the hill in the direction of the main road and I was forced to return to the ticket office for help and advice.

I found a porter, stacking hen coops in a smelly parcels office.

"I'm sorry, but I have to get to Porthkerris. Would there be a taxi?"

He shook his head slowly, without hope, and then said, brightening slightly, "There's a bus. Runs every hour." He glanced up at the slow-ticking clock high on the wall. "But you've just missed one, so you'll 'ave to wait some time."

"Can't I ring up for a taxi?"

"Isn't much call for taxis at this time of the year."

I let my heavy rucksack slip to the floor and we gazed at each other, both defeated by the enormity of the problem. My wet feet were slowly congealing. As we stood there, there came, above the noise of the storm, the sound of a car, driven very fast down the hill from the road.

I said, raising my voice slightly in order to make my point, "I must get a taxi. Where could I telephone?"

"There's a box just out there . . ."

I turned to go in search of it, trailing my rucksack behind me, and as I did so I heard the car stop outside in the yard; a door slammed, footsteps ran, and the next moment a man appeared, banging the door open and shut against the icy wind. He shook himself like a dog before crossing the floor and disappearing through the open door of the Parcels Office.

I heard him say, "Hallo, Ernie. I think there's a parcel here for me. From London."

" 'Ullo, Mr Gardner. That's a dirty night."

"Filthy. The road's awash. That looks like it . . . that one over there. Yes, that's it. Want me to sign for it?"

"Oh, yes, you'll 'ave to sign. 'Ere we are . . ."

I imagined the slip of paper, smoothed on a table top, the stub of a pencil taken from behind Ernie's ear. And for the life of me I could not remember where I had heard that voice before, nor why I knew it so well.

"That's great. Thanks very much.'

"You're welcome."

The telephone, the taxi, forgotten for the moment, I watched the door, waiting for him to reappear. When he did, carrying a large box stuck with red GLASS labels, I saw the long legs, the blue denims drenched in mud to the knee, and a black oilskin, beaded and running with rivulets of water. He was bare-headed, his black hair plastered to his skull, and he saw me for the first time and stopped dead, holding the parcel in front of him like an offering. In his dark eyes was first a flicker of puzzlement, and then recognition. He began to smile. He said, "Good God!"

It was the young man who had sold me the two little cherrywood chairs.

I stood open-mouthed, feeling obscurely that someone had played me a mean and unfair trick. If ever I was in need of a friend it was at this moment, and yet fate had chosen to send me, possibly, the last person on earth I ever wanted to see again. And that he should see me thus, drenched and desperate, was somehow the last straw.

His smile widened. "What a fantastic coincidence. What are you doing here?"

"I've just got off the train."

"Where are you going?"

I had to tell him. "To Porthkerris."

"Is someone coming for you?"

I very nearly lied and told him "yes." Anything to get rid of him. But I was always a useless fibber, and he would be bound to guess the truth. I said, "No," and then I went on, trying to sound competent, as though I could take good care of myself, "I'm just going to phone for a taxi."

"It'll take hours. I'm going to Porthkerris, I'll give you a ride."

"Oh, you don't need to bother . . ."

"No bother, I'm going anyway. Is that all your luggage?"

"Yes, but . . ."

"Come on then."

I still hesitated, but he seemed to consider the matter already settled, going over to the door to open it, and holding it open with his shoulder, waiting for me to follow. So eventually I did so, edging past him, and out into the fury of the dark evening.

In the dim light I saw the Mini pick-up, parked, with the sidelights burning. Letting the door slam behind him, he crossed over to this, and gently loaded his parcel into the back, and then took my rucksack from me, and heaved this in too, covering the two bundles in a cursory fashion with an old piece of tarpaulin. I stood watching him, but he said, "Go on, get in, there's no point us both getting wet through," so I did as I was told, settling myself in the passenger seat with my bag jammed between my legs. Almost at once he had joined me, shutting his door with an almighty slam, and switching on the engine as though there were not a moment to be lost. We roared up the hill away from the station, and the next moment had turned on to the main road and were heading for Porthkerris.

He said, "Tell me more, now. I thought you lived in London."

"Yes, I do."

"Have you come down for a holiday?"

"Sort of."

"That sounds good and vague. Are you staying with friends?"

"Yes. No. I don't know."

"What does that mean?"

"Just that. It means I don't know." This sounded rude but it couldn't be helped. I felt as though I had no control over what I was saying.

"Well, you'd better make up your mind before you get to Porthkerris, otherwise you'll be spending the night on the beach."

"I . . . I'm going to stay in a hotel. Just for tonight."

"Well, that's great. Which one?"

I sent him an exasperated look and he said, reasonably enough, "Well, if I don't know which one, I can't take you there, can I?"

He seemed to have me cornered. I said, "I haven't booked in to any hotel. I mean, I thought I could do that when I arrived. There *are* hotels, aren't there?"

"Porthkerris is running with them. Every other house is a hotel. But at this time of the year most of them are closed."

"Do you know some that are open?"

"Yes. But it depends what you want to pay."

He glanced at me sideways, taking in my patched jeans, scuffed shoes, and an old fur-lined leather coat that I had worn for warmth and comfort. At the moment this garment looked and smelt like a wet dog.

"We go from one extreme to the other. The Castle, up on the Hill, where you change for dinner, and dance the foxtrot to a three-piece orchestra, right down to Mrs Kernow who does Bed and Breakfast at Number Two, Fish Lane. Mrs Kernow I can recommend. She looked after me for three months or more before I got into my own place, and her prices are very reasonable."

I was diverted. "Your own place? You mean you live here?"

"I do now. Have done for the last six months."

"But . . . the shop in the New Kings Road . . . where I bought the chairs?"

"I was just helping out for a day or so."

We came to a crossroads, and, slowing down, he turned to look at me. "Have you got the chairs yet?"

"No. But I've paid for them. They'll still be there when I get back."

"Good," said the young man.

We drove for a little in silence. Through a village, and up over a wild bit of country high above the sea; then the road leaned down again, and there were trees on either side of us. Through these, through twisted trunks and branches tortured by the wind, there presently appeared, far below us, the twinkling lights of a little town.

"Is that Porthkerris?"

"It is. And in a moment you're going to have to tell me if it's to be The Castle or Fish Lane."

I swallowed. The Castle was out of the question, obviously, but if I went to Fish Lane I would necessarily place myself under an obligation to this managing person. I had not come to Porthkerris for any other reason than to see Grenville Bayliss, and I had an uncomfortable feeling that if I once got involved with this man he would stick like a burr.

I said, "No, not The Castle . . ." meaning to suggest some other, more modest establishment, but he cut me short.

"That's great," he said, with a grin. "Mrs Kernow of Fish Lane it is, and you won't regret it."

My first impression of Porthkerris, in the dark and the gusty rain, was confused to say the least of it. The town was, on this unsalubrious evening, nearly empty of people; the deserted streets gleamed wetly with reflected light, and the gutters ran with water.

At a great speed, we plunged down into a warren of baffling lanes and alleys, at one time emerging out on to the road which circled the harbour, only to turn back once more into the maze of cobbled roads and uneven, haphazard houses.

We turned at last into a narrow street of grey terrace houses, with front doors opening flush on to the pavement.

All was seemly and respectable. Lace curtains veiled windows, and there could be glimpsed statuettes of girls with dogs, or large green pots containing aspidistras.

The car slowed at last and stopped.

"We're here." He switched off the engine, and I could hear the wind and, above its whine, the nearby sound of the sea. Great breakers thundered up on to the sand, and there was the long hiss of the retreating waves.

He said, "You know, I don't know your name."

"It's Rebecca Bayliss. And I don't know yours."

"Joss Gardner . . . it's short for Jocelyn, not Joseph." With this useful bit of information he got out of the car and rang a bell in a door and, while waiting for an answer, went to retrieve my rucksack from underneath the tarpaulin. As he heaved it out, the door opened and he turned and was illuminated in a shaft of warm light which streamed from inside the house.

"Joss!"

"Hallo, Mrs Kernow."

"What are you doing here?"

"I've brought you a visitor. I said you were the best hotel in Porthkerris."

"Oh, my soul, I don't belong to take visitors at

this time of the year. But come along in now, out of the rain, what weather isn't it? Tom's down at the Coastguard lodge, been some sort of a warning up from the Trevose way, but I don't know, I haven't heard no rockets . . ."

Somehow we were all inside and the door shut and there was scarcely room for the three of us to stand in the narrow hall.

"Come along in by the fire . . . it's nice and warm, I'll get you a cup of tea if you like . . ." We followed her into a tiny, cluttered, cosy parlour. She knelt to poke the fire to life and add more coal, and for the first time I was able to take a good look at her. I saw a small, bespectacled lady, quite elderly, wearing bedroom slippers and a pinafore over her good brown dress.

"We don't really want tea," he told her. "We just want to know if you can give Rebecca a bed—for a night or so."

She stood up from the fireplace. "Well, I don't know . . ." She looked at me doubtfully, and what with my appearance and the dog-smelling coat I didn't blame her for being doubtful.

I started to open my mouth, but Joss sailed in before I could say a word. "She's highly respectable and she won't run away with the spoons. I'll vouch for her."

"Well . . ." Mrs Kernow smiled. Her eyes were pretty, a very pale blue. "The room's empty, so she may as well have it. But I can't give her supper tonight, not expecting anybody, I haven't anything in the house but a couple of little pasties."

"That's all right," said Joss. "I'll feed her."

I started to protest, but once again I was overborne. "I'll leave her here to get settled in and unpacked, and then I'll be back about—" he glanced at his watch—"seven thirty, to pick her up. That all right?" he flung casually in my direction. "You're an angel, Mrs Kernow, and I love you like a mother." He put an arm around her and kissed her. She looked delighted; then he gave me a final, cheerful grin, said, "See you," and so departed. We heard his car roaring away down the street.

"He's a lovely boy," Mrs Kernow informed me. "I had him living here three months or more . . . now come along, pick up your little bag and I'll show you your room. 'Course it'll be cold, but I've got an electric fire you can have, and the water in the tank's nice and hot if you want a bath . . . I always say you feel so mucky coming off those dirty trains . . ."

The room was as tiny as all the other rooms in this little house, furnished with an enormous double bed which took up nearly all the space. But it was clean and, presently, warm, and after Mrs Kernow had shown me where to find the bathroom she went back downstairs and left me to myself.

I went to kneel by the low window and draw back the curtains. The old frames had been jammed tight shut against the wind by rubber wedges, and the dark glass streamed with rain. There was nothing to be seen, but I stayed there anyway, wondering what I was doing in this little house, and trying to work out why Joss Gardner's sudden re-appearance in my life had left me with this unexplained feeling of unease.

4

I needed defences. I needed to build up my confidence and my self-esteem, disliking the role of rescued waif in which I had suddenly found myself. A hot bath and a change of clothes went a long way towards restoring my composure. I did my hair, made up my eyes, splashed on the last of a bottle of expensive scent and was halfway towards being in charge again. I had already unpacked a dress from the ubiquitous rucksack and hung it hopefully to shed its wrinkles; now I put it on, a dark cotton with long sleeves, and dark stockings, very fine, and shoes with heels and old-fashioned buckles which I had found, long back, on a stall in the Portobello Road . . . As I fastened my pearl ear-rings I heard, over the rattle and bang of the gusty wind, the sound of Joss Gardner's little van, tyres drumming on the cobbles, coming up the street. It screeched to a noisy halt outside the door, and the next moment I heard his voice downstairs, calling first for Mrs Kernow and then for me.

I continued, slowly, to screw the fastening of the

last ear-ring. I picked up my bag, and then my leather coat. This I had draped near the electric fire in the hope that it would dry off, but it hadn't. The heat had merely emphasized the smell of a spaniel come in from a wet walk, and it still weighed heavy as lead. Lugging it over my arm, I went down the stairs.

"Hallo, there." Joss, in the hall, looked up at me. "Well, what a transformation. Feel better now?"

"Yes."

"Give me your coat . . ."

He took it from me intending to help me on with it, and instantly became a comic weightlifter, sagging at the knees with the sheer bulk of it.

"You can't wear this, it'll drive you into the ground. Anyway it's still wet."

"I haven't got another." Still toting the coat, he started to laugh. My self-esteem began to drain away and some of this must have showed on my face, because he suddenly stopped laughing and shouted for Mrs Kernow. When she appeared, with an expression both exasperated and loving on her face, he bundled my coat into her arms, told her to dry it for me, unbuttoned and removed his own black oilskin and laid it, with a certain grace, around my shoulders.

Beneath it he wore a soft grey sweater, a cotton scarf knotted at the neck. "Now," he said, "we are ready to go." He opened the door, on to a curtain of rain.

I protested, "But you'll get wet," but he only said "Scuttle" so I scuttled, and he scuttled too, and the next instant we were back in the van, scarcely wet at all, with the doors banged tight and shut against the storm, although small puddles of rain on my seat and at my feet gave rise to the suspicion that this staunch vehicle was no longer as watertight as it had once been. But he started the noisy engine and we were away, and with the volume of water both outside and inside the car it was a little like being taken for a fast ride in a leaky motor boat.

I said, "Where are we going?"

"The Anchor. It's just round the corner. Not very smart. Do you mind?"

"Why should I mind?"

"You might mind. You might have wanted to be taken to The Castle."

"You mean to foxtrot to a three-piece orchestra?"

He grinned. He said, "I can't foxtrot. Nobody ever learned me."

We flashed down Fish Lane, around a right angled corner or two, beneath a stone archway and so out into a small square. One side of this was formed by the low, uneven shape of an old inn. Warm light shone from behind small windows spilled from a crooked doorway and the Inn sign over the door swung and creaked in the wind. There were four or five cars already parked outside, and Joss inserted the van neatly into a tidy space between two of them, turned off the engine, said, "One, two, three, run," and we both got out and sprinted the short distance between the car and the shelter of the porch.

There Joss shook himself slightly, brushed the rain from the soft surface of his sweater, took the oilskin off my shoulders and opened the door for me to go ahead of him.

It was warm inside, and low-ceilinged and smelt the way old pubs have always smelt. Of beer and pipe smoke and musty wood. There was a bar, with high stools, and tables around the edge of the room. Two old men were playing darts in a corner.

The barman looked up and said, "Hi, Joss." Joss put the oilskin up on a coat hook, and led me across the room to be introduced.

"Tommy, this is Rebecca. Rebecca, this is Tommy Williams. He's been here man and boy; anything you want to know about Porthkerris, or the people who live here, you come and ask Tommy."

We said, "How do you do." Tommy had grey hair and a lot of wrinkles. He looked as though he might be a fisherman in his spare time. We sat ourselves on two stools, and Joss ordered a scotch and soda for me and a scotch and water for himself, and while Tommy fixed these the two men began to talk, falling comfortably into conversation the way men in pubs always seem to.

"How are things going with you?" That was Tommy.

"Not too bad."

"When are you opening up?"

"Easter, maybe, with a bit of luck."

"Place finished is it?"

"More or less."

"Who's doing the carpentry?"

"Doing it myself."

"That'll save you something."

My attention wandered. I lit a cigarette and looked around me, liking what I saw. The two old men playing darts; a young couple, jeaned and long-haired, crouched over a table and a couple of pints of bitter, discussing, with avid and intense concentration—existentialism? Concrete painting? How they were going to pay the rent? Something. But it mattered, intensely, to both of them.

And then a party of four, older, expensively dressed, the men self-consciously casual, the women unwittingly formal. I guessed they were staying at The Castle, and out of boredom with the weather, perhaps, had come down the town for a spot of slumming. They seemed uncomfortable, as though they knew they looked out of place, and could scarcely wait to get back to the padded velvet comfort of the big hotel on the hill.

My eyes moved on around the room, and it was then that I caught sight of the dog. He was a beautiful dog, a great red setter, his coat handsome and shining, his tail a silken plume of copper fur against the grey flags of the floor. He sat very still, close to his master, and every now and then the tail would move slightly in a thump of approval, a private applause.

Intrigued, I inspected the man who appeared to own this enviable creature, and found him almost as interesting as the dog. Sitting, with an elbow on the table top, and his chin resting on his fist, he presented to me a clear and unblurred profile, almost as though he were posing for my inspection. His head was well shaped, and his hair had that thick silver-fox look of a person who has started to go grey early in life. The single eye which his profile allowed me was deep set, and darkly shadowed, the nose was long and aquiline, the mouth pleasant, the chin strongly formed. And, from the length of his wrist, emerging from a checked shirt cuff and the sleeve of a grey tweed jacket, and the way he disposed of his legs beneath the little table, I guessed that he was tall, probably over six feet.

As I watched him, he laughed suddenly at something his companion had said. This drew my attention to the other man, and I felt a shock of surprise, because, for some reason, they did not match. Where the one was slender and elegant, the other was short, fat, red of face, and dressed in a tight-fitting navy blue blazer and a shirt collar that looked as though it were about to strangle him. It was not overly warm in the pub, but there was a shine of sweat on the ruddy brow, and I saw that the dark hair had been barbered with some ingenuity, so that a long oiled lock was combed up and over, concealing what would otherwise have been a totally bald head.

The man with the dog was not smoking, but the fat man suddenly crushed out his own cigarette in the brimming ashtray on the table, as though emphasizing some point that he was making, and almost instantly reached into his pocket for a silver case and another cigarette.

But the man with the dog had decided that it was time to go. He took his hand from his chin, pushed back his shirt cuff to consult his watch, and then finished his drink. The fat man, apparently anxious to comply with the other's arrangements, hastily lit the cigarette and then tossed back his whisky. They began to get up, pushing back their chairs with a hideous scraping sound. The dog stood up, his tail swooping in exultant circles.

Standing, one so short and fat and the other so tall and slim, the two men looked more ill-assorted than ever. The thin one reached for a raincoat which had been lying across the back of his chair and slung it over his shoulders like a cloak, and then turned towards us, heading for the door. For an instant I was disappointed, because full face, his finely drawn good looks did not live up to the promise of that intriguing profile. And then I forgot about being disappointed, because he suddenly saw Joss. And Joss, perhaps sensing his presence, stopped talking to Tommy Williams and turned to see who was standing behind him. For an instant they both looked disconcerted, and then the tall man smiled, and the smile etched lines down his thin brown cheeks and creased up his eyes, and it was impossible not to be warmed by such charm.

He said, "Joss. Long time no see." His voice was pleasant and friendly.

"Hi," said Joss, not getting off his stool.

"I thought you were in London."

"No. Back again."

The creaking swing of the door caught my attention. The other man, the fat man, had quietly left. I decided that he had an urgent appointment and thought no more about it.

"I'll tell the old boy I've seen you."

"Yes. Do that."

The deep set eyes moved in my direction, and then away again. I waited to be introduced, but nothing happened. For some reason this lack of manners on Joss's part was like a slap in the face.

At last, "Well, see you around," said the tall man, and moved off.

"Sure," said Joss.

"Night, Tommy," he called to the barman as he pushed the door open and let the dog out ahead of him.

"Good night, Mr Bayliss," said the barman.

I felt my head jerk around as though someone had pulled a string. He had already disappeared, leaving the door swinging behind him. Without thinking, I slipped off the stool to go after him, but a hand caught my arm and restrained me, and I turned to find Joss holding me back. For a surprising second our eyes clashed, and then I shook myself free. Outside I heard a car start up. Now it was too late.

I said, "Who is he?"

"Eliot Bayliss."

Eliot. Roger's boy. Mollie's child. Grenville Bayliss's grandson. My cousin. My family.

"He's my cousin."

"I didn't know that."

"You know my name. Why didn't you tell him? Why did you stop me going after him?"

"You'll meet him soon enough. Tonight it's too late and too wet and too dark for family reunions."

"Grenville Bayliss is my grandfather, too."

"I thought there was probably some connection," said Joss coolly. "Have another drink."

By now I was really angry. "I don't want another drink."

"In that case, let's go and eat."

"I don't want to eat either."

I thought that I truly didn't want to. I didn't want to spend another moment with this boorish and overbearing young man. I watched him finish his drink and get down off his stool, and for an instant I thought that he was actually going to take me at my word; was going to drive me back to Fish Lane and there dump me, un-nourished. But, luckily, he did not call my bluff, simply paid for the drinks, and without a word led the way through a door at the far end of the bar, which gave on to a flight of stairs and a small restaurant. I followed him because there didn't seem to be anything else to do. Besides, I was hungry.

Most of the tables were already occupied, but a waitress saw Joss and recognized him and came over to say good evening, and led us to what was obviously the best table in the room, set in the narrow alcove of a jutting bay window. Beyond the window could be seen the shapes of rain-washed roofs, and beyond them again the liquid darkness of the harbour, a-shimmer with reflections from the street lamps on the quay and the riding lights of fishing boats.

We faced each other. I was still deeply angry and would not look at him. I sat, drawing patterns with my finger on the table mat, and listened to him ordering what I was to eat. Apparently I was not even to be allowed the right of making my own choice. I heard the waitress say, "For the young lady, too?" as though even she were surprised by his cursory behaviour, and Joss said, "Yes, for the young lady, too," and the waitress went off, and we were alone.

After a little I looked up. His dark gaze met mine, unblinking. The silence grew, and I had the ridiculous feeling that he was waiting for me to apologize to him.

I heard myself say, "If you won't let me talk to Eliot Bayliss, perhaps you'll talk about him."

"What do you want to know?"

"Is he married?" It was the first question that came into my head.

"No."

"He's attractive." Joss acknowledged this. "Does he live alone?"

"No, with his mother. They have a house up at High Cross, six miles or so from here, but about a year ago they moved into Boscarva, to be with the old man."

"Is my grandfather ill?"

"You don't know very much about your family, do you?"

"No." I sounded defiant.

"About ten years ago Grenville Bayliss had a heart attack. That's when he stopped painting. But he always appears to have had the constitution of an ox, and he made a miraculous recovery. He didn't want to leave Boscarva, and he had this couple to take care of him . . ."

"The Pettifers?"

Joss frowned. "How do you know about the Pettifers?"

"My mother told me." I thought of the long-ago tea parties by the kitchen fire. "I never imagined they'd still be there."

"Mrs Pettifer died last year, so Pettifer and your grandfather were left on their own. Grenville Bayliss is eighty now, and Pettifer can't be far behind him. Mollie Bayliss wanted them to move up to High Cross and sell Boscarva, but the old man was adamant, so in the end she and Eliot moved in with him. Without noticeable enthusiasm, I may add." He leaned back in his chair, his long clever hands resting on the edge of the table. "Your mother . . . was she called Lisa?" I nodded.

"I knew Grenville had a daughter who'd had a daughter, but the fact that you call yourself Bayliss threw me slightly."

"My father left my mother before I was born. She never used his name."

"Where's your mother now?"

"She died—just a few days ago. In Ibiza." I repeated, "Just a few days ago," because all at once it seemed like a lifetime.

"I'm sorry." I made some sort of vague gesture, because there weren't any words. "Does your grandfather know?"

"I don't know."

"Have you come to tell him?"

"I suppose I may have to." The idea of doing so was daunting.

"Does he know you're here? In Porthkerris?"

I shook my head. "He doesn't even know me. I mean we've never met. I've never been here before." I made the final admission. "I don't even know how to find his house."

"One way and another," said Joss, "you're going to give him something of a shock."

I felt anxious. "Is he very frail?"

"No, he's not frail. He's fantastically tough. But he's getting old."

"My mother says he was frightening. Is he still frightening?"

Joss made a gruesome face, doing nothing to comfort me. "Terrifying," he said.

The waitress brought our soup. It was oxtail, thick and brown and very hot. I was so hungry that I ate it right down to the bottom of the bowl without saying another word. As I finally laid down my spoon, I looked up and saw that Joss was laughing at me.

"For a girl who didn't want to eat, you haven't done so badly."

But this time I did not rise. I pushed the empty bowl away, and leaned my elbows on the table.

"How is it that you know so much about the Bayliss family?" I asked him.

Joss had not bolted his soup as I had. Now, he was taking his time, buttering a roll, being maddeningly slow.

"It's easy," he said. "I do a certain amount of work up at Boscarva."

"What sort of work?"

"Well, I restore antique furniture. And don't gape in that unattractive fashion, it does nothing for you."

"*Restore antique furniture?* You must be joking."

"I'm not. And Grenville Bayliss has a houseful of old and very valuable stuff. In his day he made a lot of money, and he invested most of it in antiques. Now, some of the things are in a shocking state of repair, not that they haven't been polished to within an inch of their lives, but ten years ago he put in central heating and that wrecks old furniture. Drawers shrink and veneers curl and crack, and legs fall off chairs. Incidentally—" he added, diverted by the memory—"it was I who mended your cherrywood chair."

"But how long have you been doing this?"

"Let's see, I left school when I was seventeen, and I'm twenty-four now, so that makes it about seven years."

"But you had to *learn* . . ."

"Oh, sure. I did joinery and carpentry first, four

years of it at a trade school in London, and then when I'd got that under my belt, I apprenticed myself for another couple of years to an old cabinet-maker down in Sussex. I lived with him and his wife, did all the dirty jobs in the workshop, learned everything I know."

I did a few sums. "That's only six years. You said seven."

He laughed. "I took a year off in the middle to travel. My parents said I was becoming parochial. My father has a cousin who runs a cattle ranch up in the Rockies, south-west Colorado. I worked as a ranch hand nine months or more." He frowned. "What are you grinning about?"

I told him. "That first time I saw you, in the shop . . . you looked like a ranch hand . . . you looked real. And somehow it annoyed me that you weren't."

He smiled. "And you know what you looked like?"

I cooled off. "No."

"The head girl of a nicely run orphanage. And that annoyed *me.*"

A small clash of swords, and once more we were on opposite sides of the fence.

I eyed him with dislike as he cheerfully finished his soup; the waitress came to take away the empty plates, and to set down a carafe of red wine. I had not heard Joss ordering the wine, but now I watched him pour two full glasses and I saw the long spade-tipped fingers; I liked the idea of them working with wood

and old and beautiful things, shaping and measuring
and oiling and coaxing into shape. I picked up the
glass of wine and against the light it glowed red as a
ruby. I said, "Is that all you're doing in Porthkerris?
Restoring Grenville Bayliss's furniture?"

"Good God, no. I'm opening a shop. I managed
to rent these premises down on the harbour six
months or so ago. I've been here, off and on, ever
since. Now, I'm trying to get it into some sort of
order before Easter, or Whitsun, or whenever the
summer business really starts."

"Is it an antique shop?"

"No, modern, furniture, glass, textiles. But antique restoring goes on in the background. I mean I
have a workroom. I also have a small pad on the top
floor which is where I now live, which is why you
were able to take over my room at Mrs Kernow's.
One day when you've decided that I'm trustworthy
you can climb the rickety stairs and I'll show it to
you."

I ignored this fresh little sally.

"If you work down here, what were you doing in
that shop in London?"

"Tristram's? I told you, he's a friend; I drop in
and see him whenever I'm up in town."

I frowned. There were so many coincidences.
Our lives seemed to be tied up in them, like a parcel
well-knotted with ends of string. I watched him finish
his wine and once more was visited with the unease
which I had known earlier in the evening. I knew I
should ask him a thousand questions, but before I

could think of one the waitress arrived at our table once more, bearing steaks and vegetables and fried potatoes and dishes of salad. I drank some wine and watched Joss, and when the waitress had gone I said, "What does Eliot Bayliss do?"

"Eliot? He runs a garage up at High Cross, specializes in highly-powered second-hand cars, Mercedes, Alfa Romeos. If you've got the right sort of cheque book he can supply you with practically anything."

"You don't like him, do you?"

"I never said I didn't like him."

"But you don't."

"Perhaps it would be nearer the mark to say he doesn't like me."

"Why?"

He looked up, his eyes dancing with amusement. "I haven't any idea. Now why don't you eat up your steak before it gets cold."

He drove me home. It was still raining and I was, all at once, deathly tired. Outside Mrs Kernow's door Joss stopped the car, but left the engine running. I thanked him and said good night and began to open the door, but before I could do so he had reached across and stopped me. I turned to look at him.

He said, "Tomorrow. Are you going to Boscarva?"

"Yes."

"I'll take you."

"I can go alone."

"You don't know where the house is, and it's a long climb up the hill. I'll pick you up in the car. About eleven?"

Arguing with him was like arguing with a steamroller. And I was exhausted. I said, "All right."

He opened the door for me and pushed it open.

"Good night, Rebecca."

"Good night."

"I'll see you in the morning."

5

The wind did not drop during that night. But when I woke, the little window of my room at Mrs Kernow's gave me sight of a square of pale blue traversed by ballooning white clouds travelling at some speed. It was very cold, but bravely I got up and dressed and went downstairs in search of Mrs Kernow. I found her outside in the little yard at the back of the house, pegging out her washing on a line. At first, battling with flailing sheets and towels, she didn't see me, but when I appeared between a shirt and a modest lock-knit petticoat she gave a great start of surprise. Her own astonishment amused her, and she shook with shrill laughter, as though the two of us were a double act on the halls.

"You gave me some shock. I thought you were still asleep! Comfortable were you? That dratted wind's still around the place, but the rain's stopped, thank heaven. Want your breakfast do you?"

"A cup of tea, perhaps."

I helped her peg out the rest of the washing and then she picked up her empty basket and led the way back indoors. I sat at the kitchen table and she boiled a kettle and began to fry bacon.

"Have a good supper last night did you? Go to The Anchor? Tommy Williams keeps a good place there, always packed, winter and summer. I heard Joss bring you home. He's a lovely boy. I missed him when he moved out. Still, I go down sometimes to his new place, clean it up a bit for him, bring his washing home and do it here. Sad, a young man like that on his own. All wrong somehow, not having someone to take care of him."

"I should think Joss could take care of himself."

"It's not right a man doing woman's work." Mrs Kernow obviously did not believe in Women's Lib. "Besides, he's busy enough working for Mr Bayliss."

"Do you know Mr Bayliss?"

"Everyone knows he. Lived here nearly fifty years now. One of the old ones, he is. And some lovely painter he was before he took ill. Used to have an exhibition every year, and all sorts used to come down from London, famous people, everybody. 'Course, lately we don't see so much of him. He can't walk up and down the hill like he used to, and it's a bit of a business Pettifer getting that great car down these narrow lanes. Besides, in the summer, you can't move for traffic and visitors. The place is teeming with them. Sometimes you'd think half the population of the country is jammed into this little town."

She flipped the bacon on to a warm plate and set it in front of me. "There now, eat that up before it gets cold."

I said, "Mrs Kernow, Mr Bayliss is my grandfather."

She stared at me, frowning. "Your grandfather?" Then, "Whose child are you?"

"Lisa's."

"Lisa's child." She reached for a chair and slowly sat down upon it. I saw that I had shocked her. "Does Joss know?"

It seemed irrelevant. "Yes, I told him last night."

"She was a lovely little girl." She stared into my face. "I can see her in you . . . except that she was so dark and you're fair. We missed her when she went, and never came back. Where is she now?"

I told her. When I had finished she said, "And Mr Bayliss doesn't know you're here?"

"No."

"You must go now. Right away. Oh, I wish I could be there to see the old man's face. He worshipped your mother . . ."

A tear gleamed. Quickly, before we were both awash with sentiment, I said, "I don't know how to get there."

Trying to tell me, she confused the two of us so much that finally she found an old envelope and the stub of a pencil and drew a rough map. Watching her I remembered Joss's promise to come at eleven o'clock and take me to Boscarva in his ramshackle van, but all at once it seemed a much better idea to go at once, on my own. Besides, last night I had been altogether too meek and compliant. It would do

Joss's boundless ego no harm to arrive here and find me already gone. The thought of this happening cheered me considerably and I went upstairs to fetch my coat.

Outside I was instantly buffeted by the wind which tunnelled down the narrow street like the draught in a chimney. It was a cold wind, smelling of the sea, but when the sun burst out from behind the racing clouds the brightness was dazzling, full of glare, and overhead gulls screamed and floated, their wings white sails against the blue of the sky.

I walked and soon I was climbing. Up narrow, cobbled streets, between haphazard lines of houses. Up flights of steps, and leaning alleys. The higher I went the stronger became the wind. As I climbed the town dropped below me, and the ocean revealed itself, dark blue, streaked with jade and purple and flecked with white horses. It spread to the horizon where the sky took over, and below me the town and the harbour shrank to toy-size, to insignificance.

I stood looking at it, catching my breath, and all at once a funny thing happened. For this new place was not new to me at all, but totally familiar. I felt at home, as though I had returned to somewhere I had known all my life. And though I had scarcely thought of my mother since making the decision to come to Porthkerris, she was suddenly beside me, climbing the steep streets, long-legged, breathless, and warm with exertion as I was.

I was comforted by this sense of *déjà-vu*. It made me feel less lonely and much more brave. I went on and was glad I had not waited for Joss. His presence was disturbing, but I could not for the life of me decide why. He had, after all, been quite open with me, answering questions, giving perfectly believable reasons for his every action.

It was obvious that there was no love lost between himself and Eliot Bayliss, but I could easily understand this. The two young men would have nothing in common. Eliot, albeit unwillingly, was living at Boscarva. He was a Bayliss and the house was, for the time being, his home. On the other hand Joss's occupation in the house would give him the freedom to come and go in his own time. Be found, unexpectedly, at odd hours of the day, perhaps when his presence was neither convenient nor welcome. I imagined him on easy terms with everybody, sometimes getting in the way, and worst of all, blithely unaware of the trouble he was causing. A man like Eliot would resent this and Joss, in return, would react to his resentment.

Busy with these thoughts and the exertion of climbing, I did not observe my surroundings, but now the road levelled off beneath my feet, and I stopped to look around and take my bearings. I was on top of the hill, that was for sure. Behind and below me lay the town; ahead stretched the rugged coastline, curving away into the distance. It bordered a green country, patchworked with small farms and miniature fields, traversed by deep valleys, thick with hawthorn and stunted elm, where narrow streams channelled their way down to the sea.

I looked about me. This too was country. Or a
year ago it had been. But since then a farm, perhaps,
had been bought out, the bulldozers brought in, old
hedges demolished, the rich earth torn up and flattened, and a new housing estate was in the process of
being erected. All was raw, stark and hideous. Ce-
ment mixers churned, a lorry ground through a sea of
mud, there were piles of brick and concrete, and in
front of it all, like a proud banner, a hoarding which
announced the man responsible for this carnage.

ERNEST PADLOW
DESIRABLE DETACHED HOUSES
FOR SALE
Apply Sea Lane, Porthkerris
Telephone Porthkerris 873

The houses were certainly detached, but only just.
Scarcely three feet lay between them, and one window stared straight into another.

My heart mourned for the lost fields and the lost
opportunities. As I stood there, mentally re-designing
the entire project, a car came up the hill behind me,
and drew to a halt in front of the hoarding. It was an
old Jaguar, navy blue, and the man who stepped out
of it, shutting the door behind him with a resounding
thump, wore a workman's donkey jacket and carried
a clip board and a lot of papers which fluttered in the
wind. He turned and saw me, hesitated for only a
second and then walked towards me, trying to flatten
his hair down over his bald head.

"Morning." His smile was familiar as though we were old friends.

"Good morning."

I had seen him before. Last night. At The Anchor. Talking to Eliot Bayliss.

He glanced up at the hoarding.

"Thinking of buying a house for yourself?"

"No."

"You should. Get a good view up here."

I frowned. "I don't want a house."

"Be a good investment."

"Are you the foreman?"

"No." He glanced, with some pride, up at the hoarding which reared above us. "I'm Ernest Padlow."

"I see."

"Lovely site this . . ." He looked around at the devastation with some satisfaction. "Lot of people after this site, but the old girl who owned the land was a widow, and I managed to charm her into letting me have it."

I was surprised. As he spoke he reached for and lit himself a cigarette; he did not offer me one, his fingers were stained with nicotine and he seemed to me the most uncharming man I had ever met.

He turned his attention back to me. "Haven't seen you around, have I?"

"No."

"Visiting?"

"Yes, perhaps."

"It's better out of season. Not so crowded."

I said, "I'm looking for Boscarva."

Caught unawares, the bonhomie slid from his manner. His eyes were sharp as pebbles in his florid face. "Boscarva? You mean old Bayliss's place?"

"Yes."

His expression became wily. "Looking for Eliot?"

"No."

He waited for me to enlarge on this. When I didn't he tried to make a joke of it. "Well, I always say, least said, soonest mended. You want Boscarva, you go down that little lane. About half a mile. You'll see the house down towards the sea. It's got a slate roof, a big garden round it. You can't miss it."

"Thank you." I smiled politely. "Goodbye."

I turned and began to walk, feeling his eyes on my back. Then he spoke once more and I turned back. He was smiling, all friends again.

"You want a house, make up your mind quickly. They're selling like hot cakes."

"Yes, I'm sure. But I don't want one. Thank you."

The lane led downhill towards the great blue bowl of the sea, and now I was truly in the country, in a farmland of fields grazed by sweet-faced Guernseys. Wild violets and primroses grew in the grassy hedges, and the sun came out and turned the rich grass to emerald. Presently, I came around a corner and saw the white gates, set between low drystone walls; a driveway curved down, out of sight, and there were high hedges of escallonia and elm trees, tortured to unnatural shapes by the relentless winds.

I could not see the house. I stood at the open gates and looked down the drive, my courage seeping away like bathwater after the plug has been pulled out. I could not think what I was meant to do, nor what I was going to say once I had done it.

My mind was, unexpectedly and mercifully, made up for me. Down by the house, out of sight, I heard a car start up and come at some speed up the drive towards me. As it approached, a low-slung open sports car of some age and style, I stood aside to let it flash past between the gate posts and up the hill in the direction from which I had come, but still there was time to see the driver and the great red setter sitting up on the back seat, with the deliriously joyful expression of any dog being taken for a ride in an open car.

I thought that I had not been noticed but I was wrong. A moment later the car stopped with a screech of brakes and a shower of small stones flung from the back wheels. Then it went into reverse, and returned, with scarcely less speed back to the spot where I stood. It stopped, the engine was killed, and Eliot Bayliss, leaning an arm on the driving wheel, surveyed me across the empty passenger seat. He was bare-headed and wore a sheepskin car coat, and his expression was one of amusement, perhaps intrigue.

"Hallo," he said.

"Good morning." I felt a fool, bundled in my

old coat, with the wind blowing stray strands of hair over my face. I tried to push them away.

"You look lost."

"No. I'm not."

He continued to regard me, frowning slightly. "I saw you last night, didn't I? At The Anchor? With Joss."

"Yes."

"Are you looking for Joss? As far as I know he's not arrived yet. That is, if he's decided to come today."

"No. I mean I'm not looking for him."

"Then who—" asked Eliot Bayliss gently—"are you looking for?"

"I . . . I wanted to see old Mr Bayliss."

"It's a little early for that. He doesn't usually appear 'til mid-day."

"Oh." I had not thought of this. Some of my disappointment must have shown in my face, for he went on, in the same gentle and friendly voice, "Perhaps I could help. I'm Eliot Bayliss."

"I know. I mean . . . Joss told me last night."

A small frown appeared between his eyebrows. He was obviously and naturally puzzled by my relationship with Joss.

"Why did you want to see my grandfather?" And when I did not reply, he suddenly leaned across to open the door of the car and said, with cool authority, "Get in."

I got in, closing the door behind me. I could feel his eyes on me, the shapeless coat, the patched jeans.

The dog leaned forward to nuzzle my ear; his nose was cold and I reached over my shoulder to stroke the long, silky ear.

I said, "What's he called?"

"Rufus. Rufus the Red. But that doesn't answer my question, does it?"

I was saved by another interruption. Another car. But this time it was the Post Office van, rattling scarlet and cheerful, down the lane towards us. It stopped, and the postman rolled down the window to say to Eliot, good naturedly, "How can I get down the drive and deliver the letters if you park your car in the gateway?"

"Sorry," said Eliot, unperturbed, and he got out from behind the driving wheel and went to take a handful of mail and a newspaper from the postman. "I'll take it—it'll save you the trip."

"Lovely," said the postman. "Be nice if everyone did my job for me," and with a grin and a wave he went on his way, presumably to some outlying farmstead.

Eliot got back into the car.

"Well," he said, smiling at me. "What am I going to do with you?"

But I scarcely heard him. The pile of mail lay loosely in his lap, and on the top was an airmail envelope, postmarked Ibiza, and addressed to Mr Grenville Bayliss. The spiky handwriting was unmistakable.

A car is a good place for confidences. There is no telephone and you can't be unexpectedly interrupted.

I said, "That letter. The one on the top. It's from a man called Otto Pedersen. He lives in Ibiza."

Eliot, frowning, took up the envelope. He turned it over and read Otto's name on the back. He looked at me. "How did you know?"

"I know his writing. I know him. He's writing to . . . to your grandfather to tell him that Lisa is dead. She died about a week ago. She was living with Otto in Ibiza."

"Lisa. You mean Lisa Bayliss?"

"Yes. Roger's sister. Your aunt. My mother."

"You're Lisa's child?"

"Yes." I turned to look directly at him. "I'm your cousin. Grenville Bayliss is my grandfather, too."

His eyes were a strange colour, greyish-green, like pebbles washed by some fast-moving stream. They showed neither shock nor pleasure, simply regarded me levelly without expression. He said at last, "Well I'll be damned."

It was hardly what I expected. We sat in silence because I could think of nothing to say, and then, as though coming to a sudden decision, he tossed the pile of mail into my lap, started the car up once more, and swung the wheel around so that once more we were facing the drive.

"What are you doing?" I asked.

"What do you think? Taking you home of course."

Home. Boscarva. We came around the curve of the drive and it was there, waiting for me. Not small, but not large either. Grey stone, smothered in creeper, grey slate roof, a semicircular stone porch with the door open to the sunshine, and inside a glimpse of red tiles, a clutter of flowerpots, the pinks and scarlets of geranium and fuchsia. A curtain fluttered at an open upstairs window and smoke plumed from a chimney. As we got out of the car the sun came out from behind a cloud and, caught in the spread arms of the house, sheltered from the north wind, it was suddenly very warm.

"Come along," said Eliot and led the way, the dog at his heels. We went through the porch and into a dark, panelled hallway illuminated by the big window on the turn of the stairs. I had imagined Boscarva as being a house of the past, sad and nostalgic, filled with the chill of old memories. But it wasn't like that at all. It was vital, humming with a sense of activity. There were papers lying on the table, a pair of gardening gloves, a dog's lead. From beyond a doorway came the kitchen sounds of voices and the clatter of crockery. From upstairs a vacuum-cleaner hummed. And there was a smell compounded of scrubbed stone and old polished floors, and years of woodfires.

Eliot stood at the foot of the staircase and called, "Mamma." But when there was no answer, only the continued hum of the vacuum-cleaner, he said, "You'd better come this way." We went down the hall and through a door which led into a long, low drawing room, palely panelled and sensuous with the brightness and scent of spring flowers. At one end, in a fireplace of carved pine and Dutch tiles, a newly lit fire flickered cheerfully, and three tall windows, curtained in faded yellow silk, faced out over a flagged terrace, and beyond the balustrade of this I could see the blue line of the sea.

I stood in the middle of this charming room as Eliot Bayliss closed the door and said, "Well, you're here. Why don't you take your coat off?"

I did so. It was very warm. I laid it over a chair where it looked like some great, dead creature.

He said, "When did you get here?"

"Last night. I caught the train from London."

"You live in London?"

"Yes."

"And you've never been here before?"

"No. I didn't know about Boscarva. I didn't know about Grenville Bayliss being my grandfather. My mother never told me till the night before she died."

"How does Joss come into it?"

"I . . ." It was too complicated to explain. "I'd met him in London. He happened to be at the junction when my train got in. It was a coincidence."

"Where are you staying?"

"With Mrs Kernow in Fish Lane."

"Grenville's an old man. He's ill. You know that, don't you?"

"Yes."

"I think . . . this letter from Otto Pedersen . . . we'd better be careful. Perhaps my mother would be the best person . . ."

"Yes, of course."

"It was lucky you saw the letter."

"Yes. I thought he would probably write. But I was afraid that I would have to break the news to you all."

"And now it's been done for you." He smiled, and all at once he looked much younger . . . belying those strange coloured eyes and the thick silver-fox hair. "Why don't you wait here and I'll go and find my mother and try to put her in the picture. Would you like a cup of coffee or something?"

"Only if it's not a nuisance."

"No nuisance. I'll tell Pettifer." He opened the door behind him. "Make yourself at home."

The door closed softly, and he was gone. Pettifer. *Pettifer had been in the Navy too, he looked after my father and sometimes drove the car and Mrs Pettifer did the cooking.* So my mother had told me. And Joss had told me that Mrs Pettifer had died. But in the old days she had taken Lisa and her brother into the kitchen and made hot buttered toast. She had drawn the curtains against the dark and the rain, and made the children feel safe and loved.

Alone, I inspected the room where I had been left to wait. I saw a glass-doored cabinet filled with Oriental treasures, including some small pieces of jade, and wondered if these were the ones that my mother had mentioned to me. I glanced around, thinking that perhaps I might find the Venetian mirror and the davenport desk as well, but then my attention was caught by the picture over the mantelpiece, and I went to look at it, all else forgotten.

It was a portrait of a girl, dressed in the fashion of the early 1930s, slender, flat-chested, her white dress hanging straight to her hips, her dark, bobbed hair revealing with enchanting innocence the long, slender neck. She sat, in the picture, on a tall stool, holding a single long-stemmed rose, but you could not see her face, for she was looking away from the artist, out of some unseen window, into the sunshine. The effect was all pink and gold, with sunlight filtering through the thin stuff of her white dress. It was enchanting.

Behind me the door opened suddenly and I turned, startled, as an old man came into the room, stately, bald-headed, a little stooped, perhaps; treading cautiously. He wore rimless spectacles and a striped shirt with an old-fashioned hard collar, and over it all a blue and white butcher's apron.

"Are you the young lady wanting a cup of coffee?" He had a deep, lugubrious voice, and this, with his sombre appearance, made me think of a reliable undertaker.

"Yes, if it's not too much trouble."

"Milk and sugar?"

"No sugar. Just a little milk. I was looking at the portrait."

"Yes. It's very pleasing. It's called 'Lady Holding a Rose'."

"You can't see her face."

"No."

"Did my . . . Did Mr Bayliss paint it?"

"Oh yes. That was hung in the Academy, could have been sold a hundred times over, but the Commander would never part with it." As he said this, he carefully took off his spectacles, and was now staring at me intently. His old eyes were pale. He said, "For a moment, when you spoke, you reminded me of someone else. But you're young and she'd be middle-aged by now. And her hair was dark as a blackbird. That's what Mrs Pettifer used to say. Dark as a blackbird's wing."

I said, "Eliot didn't tell you?"

"What didn't Mr Eliot tell me?"

"You're talking about Lisa, aren't you? I'm Rebecca. I'm her daughter."

"Well." Fumbling a little he put his spectacles back on again. A faint gleam of pleasure showed on his gloomy features. "I was right then. I'm not often wrong about things like that." And he came forward, holding out a horny hand. "It's a real pleasure to meet you . . . A pleasure that I never thought I should have. I thought you'd never come. Is your mother with you?"

I wished that Eliot had made it a little easier for me.

"My mother's dead. She died last week. In Ibiza. That's why I'm here."

"She died." His eyes clouded. "I'm sorry. I'm really sorry. She should have come back. She should have come home. We all wanted to see her again." He took out a copious handkerchief and blew his nose.

"And who—" he asked— "is going to tell the Commander?"

"I think . . . Eliot's gone to fetch his mother. You see, there's a letter for my grandfather in the post, it came this morning. It's from Ibiza, from the man who was . . . taking care of my mother. But if you think that wouldn't be a very good idea . . ."

"What I think won't make no difference," said Pettifer. "And whoever tells the Commander, it's not going to lessen his sorrow. But I'll tell you one thing. You being here will help a lot."

"Thank you."

He blew his nose again and put away his handkerchief.

"Mr Eliot and his mother . . . well, this isn't their home. But it was either the old Commander and me moving up to High Cross or them coming here. And they wouldn't be here if the doctor hadn't insisted. I told them we could manage all right, the Commander and me. We've been together all these years . . . but there, we're neither of us as young as we used to be, and the Commander, he had this heart attack . . ."

"Yes, I know . . ."

"And after Mrs Pettifer passed on, there wasn't anyone to do the cooking. Mind, I can cook all right, but it takes me a good part of my time taking care of the Commander, and I wouldn't want to see him going about the place looking shabby."

"No, of course not . . ."

I was interrupted by the slam of a door.

A hearty male voice called, "Pettifer!" and Pettifer said, "Excuse me a moment, miss," and went out to investigate, leaving the door open behind him.

"Pettifer!"

I heard Pettifer say, with what sounded like the greatest satisfaction, "Hallo, Joss."

"Is she there?"

"Who, here?"

"Rebecca."

"Yes, she's right here, in the sitting-room . . . I was just going to get her a cup of coffee."

"Make it two would you, there's a good chap. And black and strong for me."

His footsteps came down the hall, and the next moment he was there, framed in the doorway, long-legged, black-haired, and—it was obvious—angry.

"What the hell do you think you're doing?" he demanded.

I could feel my hackles rising, like a suspicious dog. Home, Eliot had said. This was Boscarva, my home, and whether I was here or not was nothing to do with Joss.

"I don't know what you're talking about."

"I went to pick you up and Mrs Kernow told me you'd already left."

"So?"

"I told you to wait for me."

"I decided not to wait."

He was silent, fuming, but finally appeared to accept this inescapable fact.

"Does anyone know you've arrived?"

"I met Eliot at the gate. He brought me here."

"Where's he gone?"

"To find his mother."

"Have you seen anyone else? Have you seen Grenville?"

"No."

"Has anyone told Grenville about your mother?"

"A letter came by this morning's post, from Otto Pedersen. But I don't think he's seen it yet."

"Pettifer must take it to him. Pettifer must be there when he reads it."

"Pettifer didn't seem to think that."

"I think it," said Joss.

His apparently outrageous interference left me without words, but as we stood glaring at each other across the pretty patterned carpet and a great bowl of scented narcissus, there came the sound of voices and footsteps down the uncarpeted staircase and along the hall towards us.

I heard a woman's voice say, "In the sitting-room, Eliot?"

Joss muttered something that sounded unprintable, and marched over to the fireplace where he stood with his back to me, staring down into the flames. The next instant, Mollie appeared in the doorway, hesitated for a moment and then came towards me, hands outstretched.

"Rebecca." (So it was to be a warm welcome.) Eliot, following behind her, closed the door. Joss did not even turn round.

I worked it out that by now Mollie must be over fifty, but this was hard to believe. She was plump and pretty, her fading blonde hair charmingly coiffed, her eyes blue, her skin fresh and lightly scattered with freckles which helped to create this astonishing illusion of youth. She wore a blue skirt and cardigan and a creamy silk blouse; her legs were slim and shapely and her hands beautifully manicured, decorated with pale pink fingernails, and many rings and fine gold bracelets. Scented, immaculately preserved, she made me think of a charming little tabby cat, curled precisely in the centre of her own satin cushion.

I said, "I'm afraid this is something of a shock."

"No, not a shock, but a surprise. And your mother . . . I'm so dreadfully sorry. Eliot's told me about the letter . . ."

At this Joss swung around from the fireplace.

"Where is the letter?"

Mollie turned her gaze upon him, and it was impossible to guess whether this was the first time she had realized he was there, or whether she had seen him and simply decided to ignore him.

"Joss. I didn't think you were coming this morning."

"Yes. I just got here."

"You know Rebecca, I believe."

"Yes, we've met." He hesitated, seeming to be making an effort to pull himself together. Then he smiled, ruefully, turned to lean his broad shoulders against the mantelpiece and apologized. "I'm sorry.

And I know it's none of my business, but that letter that came this morning . . . where is it?"

"In my pocket," said Eliot, speaking for the first time. "Why?"

"It's just that I think Pettifer should be the one to break the news to the old man. I think Pettifer is the only person to do it."

This was greeted by silence. Then Mollie let go of my hands and turned to her son.

"He's right," she said. "Grenville's closest to Pettifer."

"That's all right by me," said Eliot, but his eyes, on Joss, were cold with antagonism. I did not blame him. I felt the same way myself—I was on Eliot's side.

Joss said again, "I'm sorry."

Mollie was polite. "Not at all. It's very thoughtful of you to be so concerned."

"None of my business, really," said Joss. Eliot and his mother waited with pointed patience. At last he took the hint, heaved his shoulders away from the mantelpiece, and said, "Well, if you'll excuse me, I'll go and get on with some work."

"Will you be here for lunch?"

"No, I can only stay a couple of hours. I'll have to get back to the shop. I'll pick up a sandwich at the pub." He smiled benignly at us all, not a trace of his former temper showing. "Thanks all the same."

And so he left us, modest, apologetic, apparently cut down to size. Once more the young workman, an employee, with a job to do.

6

Mollie said, "You must forgive him. He's not always the most tactful of men."

Eliot laughed shortly. "That's the understatement of the year."

She turned to me, explaining, "He's restoring some of the furniture for us. It's old and it had got into bad repair. He's a marvellous craftsman, but we never know when he's going to arrive or when he's going to go!"

"One day," said her son, "I shall lose my temper with him and punch his nose into the back of his neck." He smiled at me charmingly, his eyes crinkling, belying the ferocity of his words. "And I'm going to have to go too. I was late as it was, now I'm bloody late. Rebecca, will you excuse me?"

"Of course. I'm sorry, I'm afraid it was my fault. And thank you for being so kind . . ."

"I'm glad I stopped. I must have known how important it was. I'll see you . . ."

"Yes, of course you will," said Mollie quickly "She can't go away now that she's found us."

"Well I'll leave the two of you to fix everything up . . ." He made for the door, but his mother interrupted gently.

"Eliot." He turned. "The letter."

"Oh, yes, of course." He took it from his pocket, the fateful letter, a little crumpled now, and handed it to Mollie. "Don't let Pettifer make too big a meal of it. He's a sentimental old chap."

"I won't."

He smiled again, saying goodbye to both of us. "See you at dinner."

And he was gone, whistling up his dog as he went down the hall. We heard the front door open and shut, his car start up. Mollie turned to me.

"Now," she said, "come and sit by the fire and tell me all about it."

I did so, as I had already told Joss and Mrs Kernow, only this time I found myself stumbling a little when I got to the bit about Otto and Lisa living together, as though I were ashamed of it, which was a thing which I had never been. As I talked and Mollie listened, I tried to work this out, and to understand why my mother had disliked her so much. Perhaps it was simply a natural antipathy. It was obvious that they would never have had anything in common. And my mother had never had much tolerance for women who bored her. Men, now, were different. Men were always amusing. But women had to be very special for my mother to be able to tolerate their company. No, it could not all have been Mollie's fault. Sitting across the fireside from her, I resolved that I would be friends with her, and perhaps compensate, in a small way, for the short shrift she had received from Lisa.

"And how long are you going to be able to stay in Porthkerris? Your job . . . do you have to get back?"

"No. I seem to have been given a sort of indefinite leave."

"You'll stay here, with us?"

"Well, I've got this room with Mrs Kernow."

"Yes, but you'd be much better here. There's not a lot of space, that's the only thing; you'll have to sleep up in the attic, but it's a dear little room if you don't mind the sloping ceilings and you manage not to bump your head. You see, Eliot and I seem to have filled up the guest rooms, and as well I've got my niece staying for a few days. Perhaps you'll make friends with her. It'll be nice for her to have someone young about the place."

I wondered where the niece was. "How old is she?"

"Only seventeen. It's a difficult age, and I think that her mother felt it would be a good thing if she was out of London for a little. They live there, you see, and of course she has so many friends, and there is so much going on . . ." She was obviously finding it difficult to find the right words . . . "Anyway, Andrea's down here for a week or two to have a little change, but I'm afraid she's rather bored."

I imagined myself at seventeen, in the unseen Andrea's shoes, staying in this warm and charming house, cared for by Mollie and Pettifer, with the sea and the cliffs on my doorstep, the countryside inviting long walks, and all the secret crooked streets of Porthkerris waiting to be explored. To me it would have been heaven, and impossible to be bored. I wondered if I would have very much in common with Mollie's niece.

"Of course," she went on, "as you've probably gathered, Eliot and I are only here because Mrs Pettifer died and really the two old men couldn't manage on their own. We've got Mrs Thomas, she comes in each morning to help do the housework, but I do all the cooking, and keep the place as bright and pretty as I can."

"The flowers are so lovely."

"I can't bear a house without flowers."

"What about your own house?"

"My dear, it's empty. I shall have to take you up to High Cross one day to show it to you. I bought a pair of old cottages just after the war and converted them. Even though I shouldn't say so, it is very charming. And, of course, it's so handy for Eliot's garage; as it is, living here, he seems to be perpetually on the road."

"Yes, I suppose so."

I could hear footsteps coming down the hall again; in a moment the door opened, and Pettifer edged around it, cautiously, carrying a tray laden with all the accoutrements of mid-morning coffee, including a large silver pot with steam drifting from its spout.

"Oh, Pettifer, thank you . . ."

He came forward, stooped with the weight of the tray, and Mollie got up to fetch a stool and place it swiftly beneath the tray so that the old man could put it down before it tilted so sharply that everything on it went hurtling to the floor.

"That's splendid, Pettifer."

"One of the cups was for Joss."

"He's upstairs working. He must have forgotten about the coffee. Never mind, I'll drink it for him. And, Pettifer . . ." He straightened, slowly, as though all his old joints were aching. Mollie took the letter from Ibiza off the mantelpiece where she had placed it for safety. "We thought, all of us, that perhaps it would be the best if you told the Commander about his daughter and then gave him this letter. It would be best, we thought, coming from you. Would you mind?"

Pettifer took the thin blue envelope.

"No, Madam. I'll do it. I'm just on my way up now to get the Commander up and dressed."

"It would be a kindness, Pettifer."

"That's all right, Madam."

"And tell him that Rebecca is here. And that she's staying. We'll have to make up the bed in the attic but I think she'll be quite comfortable."

Again a gleam came into Pettifer's face. I wondered if he ever really smiled, or whether his face had dropped permanently into those lugubrious lines and a cheerful expression had become physically impossible.

"I'm glad you're staying," he said. "The Commander will like that."

When he'd gone, I said, "You'll have a lot to do. Shouldn't I go, and get out from under your feet?"

"You'll have to collect your things from Mrs Kernow anyway. I wonder how we could manage that? Pettifer could take you, but now he'll be occupied with Grenville and I must speak to Mrs Thomas about your room and then start thinking about lunch. Now what are we going to do?" I could not imagine. I was certainly not going to be able to carry all my belongings up the hill from the town. But luckily Mollie answered her own question. "I know. Joss. He can take you and bring you back up the hill in his van."

"But isn't Joss working?"

"Oh, for once we'll interrupt him. It's not often he's asked to put himself out—I'm sure he won't mind. Come along, we'll go and find him."

I had thought that she would take me to some forgotten outhouse or shed where we would find Joss, surrounded by wood shavings and the smell of hot glue, but to my surprise, she led me upstairs, and I forgot about Joss, because these were my first impressions of Boscarva, where my mother had been brought up, and I didn't want to miss a thing. The stairs were uncarpeted, the walls half panelled and then darkly papered above and hung with heavy oil paintings. All was at variance with the pretty, feminine sitting-room which we had left downstairs. On the first-floor landing passages led to left and right, there was a tallboy of polished walnut, and bookcases heavy with books, and then we went on again, up the stairs. Here was red drugget, white paint, again the passages led away to either side, and Mollie took the right-hand one. At the end of this passage was an open door, and from behind it the sound of voices, a man's and a girl's.

She seemed to hesitate and then her footsteps quickened, determined. Her back view became, all at once, formidable. With me following she went down the passage and through the door, and we were in an attic which had been converted, by means of a sky-light, to a studio, or perhaps a billiard room, for against one wall was a massive, leather-seated sofa with oaken arms and legs. Now, however, this cold and airy room was being used as a workshop, with Joss in the middle of it, surrounded by chairs, broken picture frames, a table with a crooked leg, some scraps of leather, tools and nails, and a gimcrack gas ring on which reposed an unsavoury-looking glue pot. Wrapped in a worn blue apron, he was carefully fitting beautiful scarlet hide over the seat of one of the chairs, and as he did this, was being entertained by a young and female companion, who turned, disinterested, to see who had come into the room, and was so breaking up this cosy *tête-à-tête*.

Mollie said, "Andrea!" And then, less sharply, "Andrea, I didn't realize you were up."

"Oh, I've been up for hours."

"Did you have any breakfast?"

"I didn't want any."

"Andrea, this is Rebecca. Rebecca Bayliss."

"Oh, yes," she turned her eyes on to me. "Joss has been telling me all about you."

I said, "How do you do." She was very young and very thin, with long seaweedy hair that hung on either side of her face, which was pretty, except for her eyes which were pale and slightly protuberant, and not improved by a great deal of clumsy mascara. She wore, inevitably, jeans, and a cotton tee-shirt which did not look entirely clean and which revealed, with no shadow of a doubt, the fact that she wore nothing beneath it. On her feet were sandals which looked like surgical boots that had been striped in green and purple. There was a leather bootlace around her neck upon which hung a heavy silver cross of vaguely Celtic design. Andrea, I thought. So bored with Boscarva. And it made me uncomfortable to think that she and Joss had been discussing me. I wondered what he had said.

Now, she did not move, but stayed where she was, legs straddled, leaning against a heavy old mahogany table.

"Hi," she said.

"Rebecca's going to stay here," Mollie told them. Joss looked up, his mouth full of tacks, his eyes bright with interest, a lock of black hair falling over his forehead.

"Where's she going to sleep?" asked Andrea. "I thought we were a full house."

"In the bedroom along the passage," her aunt told her crisply. "Joss, would you do a favour for me?" He spat the tacks neatly into his palm and stood up, pushing his hair back with his wrist. "Would you take her, now, down to Mrs Kernow, and tell Mrs Kernow that she's coming here, and then help her with her suitcases and bring her back up to Boscarva again? Would that be very inconvenient?"

"Not at all," said Joss, but Andrea's face assumed an expression of bored resignation.

"It's a nuisance, I know, when you're busy, but it would be such a help . . ."

"It's no trouble." He laid down his little hammer and began to untie the knot of his apron. He grinned at me. "I'm getting quite used to carting Rebecca about."

And Andrea gave a snort, whether of disgust or impatience it was impossible to tell, sprang to her feet and marched out of the room, leaving the impression that we had been lucky to escape without a monumentally slammed door.

And so I was back where I started, with Joss, crammed into the ramshackle little van. We drove in silence away from Boscarva, through Mr Padlow's building estate, and on to the slope of the hill that led down to the town.

It was Joss who broke the silence.

"So, it all worked out."

"Yes."

"How do you like your family?"

"I haven't met them all yet. I haven't met Grenville."

He said, "You'll like him," but the way he said it, he made it sound. "You'll like *him*."

"I like them all."

"That's good."

I looked at him. He wore his blue denim jacket, a navy polo-necked sweater. His profile was impassive. I felt it would be easy to be maddened by him.

"Tell me about Andrea," I said.

"What do you want to know about Andrea?"

"I don't know. I just want you to tell me."

"She's seventeen, and she thinks she's in love with some guy she met at Art School, and her parents don't approve so she's been rusticated with Auntie Mollie. And she's bored stiff."

"She seems to have taken you into her confidence."

"There's no one else to talk to."

"Why doesn't she go back to London?"

"Because she's only seventeen. She hasn't got the money. And I think she hasn't quite got the courage to stand up to her parents."

"What does she do with herself all day?"

"I don't know. I'm not there all day. She doesn't seem to get up until lunchtime, and then she sits around watching television. Boscarva's a house of old people. You can't blame her for being bored."

I said, without thinking, "Only the boring are bored." This had once been drummed into me by a wise and well-meaning headmistress.

"That," said Joss, "sounds uncomfortably sanctimonious."

"I didn't mean it to."

He smiled. "Were you never bored?"

"Nobody who lived with my mother was ever bored."

He sang, "You may have been a headache, but you never were a bore."

"Exactly."

"She sounds great. Exactly my sort of female."

"That's what most men thought about her."

When we got to Fish Lane Mrs Kernow was out, but Joss seemed to have a key. We let ourselves in and I went upstairs to pack my suitcase and my rucksack while Joss wrote Mrs Kernow a note to explain the new arrangements.

"How about paying her?" I asked as I came downstairs, bumping the rucksack behind me.

"I'll fix that when I next see her. I've told her so in the note."

"But I can pay for myself."

"Of course you can, but let me do it for you." He took my suitcase and went to open the door, and there did not seem to be opportunity for further argument.

Once more my belongings were heaved into the back of the little truck, once more we headed for Boscarva, only this time Joss took me round by the harbour road.

"I want to show you my shop . . . I mean, I

just want to show you where it is. Then if you want to get hold of me for any reason, you'll know where to find me."

"Why should I want to get hold of you?"

"I don't know. You might need wise counselling; or money; or just a good laugh. There it is, you can't miss it."

It was a tall narrow house, boxed in between two short fat houses. Three storeys high with a window on each floor, and the ground floor still in a state of reconstruction, with new wood unpainted and great circles of whitewash splashed over the plate glass of the shop window.

As we flashed past it, tyres rattling on the cobbles, I said, "That's a good position, you'll get all the visitors coming in to spend their money."

"That's what I hope."

"When can I see it?"

"Come next week. We'll be more or less straight then."

"All right. Next week."

"It's a date," said Joss, and turned the corner by the church. He put the little truck into second gear and we roared up the hill with a noise like a badly tuned motor bicycle.

Back at Boscarva, it was Pettifer who, hearing our arrival, emerged from the front door as Joss lifted my suitcase from the back of the truck.

"Joss, the Commander's downstairs and in his study. He said to bring Rebecca in to see him just as soon as you arrived."

Joss looked at him. "How is he?"

Pettifer ducked his head. "Not too bad."

"Was he very upset?"

"He's all right . . . now you leave that case, and I'll carry it upstairs."

"You'll do no such thing," said Joss, and for once I was glad that he was being his usual bossy self. "I'll take it up. Where's she sleeping?"

"In the attic . . . the other end from the billiard room, but the Commander did say, right away."

"I know," Joss grinned, "and Naval time is five minutes beforehand. But there's still time to take the girl up to her room, so stop fussing, there's a good man."

Leaving Pettifer still mildly protesting, I followed him up the two flights of stairs that I had already climbed this morning. The sound of the vacuum had stopped, but there was the smell of roasting lamb. I realized then that I was very hungry and my mouth watered. Joss's long legs sped ahead of me, and by the time I reached the slope-ceilinged bedroom which was to be mine, he had set down the suitcase and the rucksack and gone to fling wide the dormer window, so that I was met by a blast of cold, salty air.

"Come and look at the view."

I went to stand beside him. I saw the sea, the cliffs, the gold of bracken and the first yellow candles of gorse. And below was the Boscarva garden which, because of the stone balustrade of the terrace, I had not been able to see from the drawing-room window.

It had been built in a series of terraces, dropping down the slope of the hill, and at the bottom, tucked into a corner of the garden wall, was a stone cottage with a slate roof. No, not a cottage, perhaps a stable, with a commodious loft above it.

I said, "What's that building?"

"That's the studio," Joss told me. "That's where your grandfather used to paint."

"It doesn't look like a studio."

"From the other side it does. The entire north wall is made of glass. He designed it himself, had it built by a local stonemason."

"It looks shut up."

"It is. Locked and shuttered. It hasn't been opened since he had his heart attack and stopped painting."

I shivered suddenly.

"Cold?" asked Joss.

"I don't know." I moved away from the window, undoing my coat, dropping it over the end of the bed. The room was white, the carpet dark red. There was a built-in wardrobe, shelves full of books, a washbasin. I went over to wash my hands, turning the soap beneath the warm water. Over the basin was a mirror which gave me back a reflection both dishevelled and anxious. I realized then how nervous I was of meeting Grenville for the first time, and how important it was that he should get a good impression of me.

I dried my hands, went to unbuckle my rucksack, and found a brush and comb. "Was he a good painter, Joss? Do you think he was a good artist?"

"Yes. The old school, of course, but magnificent. And a marvellous colourist."

I pulled the rubber band from the end of my plait, shook the coils free, and went back to the mirror to start brushing. Over my reflected shoulder I could see Joss watching me. He did not speak while I brushed and combed and finally re-plaited my hair. As I fastened the ends, he said, "It's a wonderful colour. Like corn."

I laid down the brush and comb. "Joss, we mustn't keep him waiting."

"Do you want me to come with you?"

"Please."

I realized then that this was the first time I had ever had to ask him to help me.

I followed him downstairs, down the hall and past the sitting-room, to a door which stood at the end of the passage. Joss opened it and put his head around.

He said, "Good morning."

"Who's that? Joss? Come along in . . ." The voice was higher pitched than I had imagined, more like the voice of a much younger man.

"I've brought someone to see you . . ."

He opened the door wide, and put his arms behind me to propel me gently forward into the room. It was a small room, with french windows leading out on to a paved terrace and a secret garden, warm with trapped sunshine, and enclosed by dense hedges and escallonia.

I saw the fire flickering in the grate; the panelled walls covered either with pictures or books; the model, on the mantelpiece, of an old-fashioned naval cruiser. There were photographs in silver frames, a table littered with papers and magazines, and a blue and white Chinese bowl filled with daffodils.

As I entered, he was already heaving himself— with the aid of a stick—out of a red leather arm- chair, which stood half turned towards the warmth of the fire. I was amazed that Joss did nothing to help him, and I began to say, "Oh, please don't bother . . ." but by then he was on his feet and erect, and a pair of blue eyes surveyed me calmly from beneath jutting brows and bristling white eye- brows.

I realized then that I had steeled myself to find- ing him pathetic in some way, old, infirm, perhaps a little shaky. But Grenville Bayliss, at eighty, was for- midable. Very tall, very upright, starched and barbered, smelling faintly of Bay Rum, he was a credit to his servant Pettifer. He wore a dark blue blazer, of Naval cut, neatly creased grey flannels, and velvet slippers with his initials embroidered in gold. He was also very tanned, his bald head brown as a chestnut beneath the thinning strands of white hair, and I imagined him spending much time in that little sunny secret garden, reading his morning paper, en- joying a pipe, watching the gulls and the white clouds scudding across the sky.

We looked at each other. I wished that he would say something but he simply looked. I hoped that he liked what he saw, and was glad I had taken the time to brush my hair. And then he said, "I've never been in this situation before. I'm not quite sure how we're meant to greet each other."

I said, "I could give you a kiss."

"Why don't you do that?"

So I did, stepping forward and raising my face, and he stooped slightly and my lips touched the smooth clean skin of his cheek.

"Now," he said, "why don't we sit down? Joss, come and sit down."

But Joss excused himself, said that if he didn't start work soon then he would have done nothing all day. But he stayed long enough to help the old man back into his chair, and pour us both a glass of sherry from the decanter on the side table, and then he said, "I'll leave you. You'll have a lot to talk about," and with a cheerful wave of his hand, slipped away. The door closed quietly behind him.

Grenville said, "I believe you know him quite well."

I pulled up a stool so that I could sit and face him. "Not really. But he's been very kind, and . . ." I tried to think of the right word. "Convenient. I mean, he always seems to be there when people need him."

"And never when they don't?" I was not sure if I could entirely agree with this. "He's a clever boy, too. Doing up all my furniture."

"Yes, I know."

"Good craftsman. Lovely hands." He laid down his sherry glass, and once more I was subjected to that piercing blue stare. "Your mother died."

"Yes."

"Had a letter from this Pedersen fellow. He said it was leukaemia."

"Yes."

"Did you meet him?"

I told him about going to Ibiza and the night I had spent with Otto and my mother.

"He was a decent chap, then? Good to her?"

"Yes. He was immensely kind. And he adored her."

"Glad she ended up with somebody decent. Most of the chaps she picked on were just a lot of bounders."

I smiled at the old-fashioned word. I thought of the sheep-farmer, and the American in his Brooks Brothers shirts, and wondered how they would have liked being called bounders. They probably wouldn't even have known what it meant.

I said, "I think she sometimes got a little carried away."

A gleam of humour showed in his eyes. "You seem to have adopted a fairly worldly attitude?"

"Yes. I did. Long ago."

"She was a maddening woman. But she'd been the most enchanting little girl it was possible to imagine. I painted her often. I've still got one or two canvases of Lisa as a child. I'll have to get Pettifer to look them out, show them to you. And then she grew up and everything changed. Roger, my son, was killed in the war, and Lisa was always at loggerheads with her mother, rushing off in her little car, never coming home at night. Finally she fell in love with this actor fellow, and that was it."

"She really *was* in love with him."

"In love." He sounded disgusted. "That's an overrated expression. There's a lot more to life than just being in love."

"Yes, but you have to find that out for yourself."

He looked amused. "Have you found it out?"

"No."

"How old are you?"

"Twenty-one."

"You're mature for twenty-one. And I like your hair. You don't look like Lisa. You don't look like your father either. You look like yourself." He reached for his sherry glass, raised it carefully to his mouth, took a sip, and then replaced the glass on the table by his chair. In such cautious actions did he betray his age and his infirmity.

He said, "She should have come back to Boscarva. At any time we would have welcomed her. Come to that, why didn't *you* come?"

"I didn't know about Boscarva. I didn't know about you until the night before she died."

"It was as though she'd put the past out of her life. And when her mother died and I wrote to tell her, she never even replied."

"We were in New York that Christmas. She

didn't get your letter till months later. And then it seemed too late to write. And she was so bad at writing letters."

"You're standing up for her. You don't resent the fact that she kept you from this place? You could have been brought up here. This could have been your home."

"She was my mother. That was the important thing."

"You seem to be arguing with me. Nobody argues with me nowadays. Not even Pettifer. It gets very dull." Once more I was fixed with that blue stare. "Have you met Pettifer? He and I were in the Navy together about a century ago. And Mollie and Eliot? Have you met them?"

"Yes."

"They shouldn't be living here at all, of course, but the doctor insisted. Doesn't make that much difference to me, but it's hard luck on poor Pettifer. And Mollie's got a niece here as well, dreadful child with sagging breasts. Have you seen her?"

I managed not to giggle. "Yes, for a moment."

"A moment would be too long. And Boscarva. What do you think of Boscarva?"

"I love it. What I've seen of it, I love."

"The town's creeping out over the hill. There was a farm at the top, belonged to an old lady called Mrs Gregory. But this builder fellow talked her into selling up to him and now they've bulldozed the fields flat as a pancake and they're putting up houses nineteen to the dozen."

"I know. I saw them."

"Well, they can't come any further, because the farm at the back of this place and the fields on either side of the lane belong to me. Bought them when I bought Boscarva, back in 1922. Wouldn't like to tell you how little it cost me. But a bit of land around you gives you a feeling of security. Remember that."

"I will."

He frowned. "What's your name again? I've forgotten it already."

"Rebecca."

"Rebecca. And what are you going to call me?"

"I don't know. What do you want me to call you?"

"Eliot calls me Grenville. You call me Grenville too. It sounds more friendly."

"All right."

We drank our sherry, smiling, content with each other. Then, from the back of the house, came the sound of a gong being rung. Grenville put down his glass and got painfully to his feet, and I went to open the door for him. Together, we went down the passage towards the dining room and family lunch.

7

Exhaustion hit me at the end of that long, eventful day, and unfortunately in the middle of dinner. Luncheon had been a sustaining, homely meal, eaten at a round table set in the bay window of the big dining room. This had been laid with a simple checked cloth, and everyday china and glass, but dinner was a different affair altogether.

The long, polished table in the middle of the room was set for the five of us, with fine linen mats, and old silver and glass sparkling in the candlelight.

Everybody, it seemed, was expected to change in honour of this apparently nightly ritual. Mollie came downstairs in a brocade housecoat the colour of sapphires, which emphasized the brightness of her eyes. Grenville wore a faded velvet dinnerjacket and Eliot a pale flannel suit in which he looked as elegant as a greyhound. Even Andrea, probably under much protest, had put on a different pair of trousers and a blouse of broderie anglaise which looked as though it could have done with a press, or a wash, or maybe both. Her lank hair was tied back with a scrap of velvet ribbon, the expression on her face continued to be one of resentful boredom.

Not in the habit of attending formal dinner parties, I had nevertheless packed a garment which would obviously have to appear every evening as long as I stayed in this house, for I had no other. It was a caftan of soft brown jersey wool, with silver embroidery at the neck and the wrists of the flowing sleeves. With it, I wore my silver bracelets and a pair of hoop ear-rings which my mother had given me for my twenty-first birthday. Their weight, on this occasion, gave me odd comfort and confidence, two things which I badly needed.

I did not want to have dinner with my newly acquired family. I did not want to have to make conversation, to listen, to be intelligent and charming. I wanted to go to bed and be brought something undemanding, like Bovril or a boiled egg. I wanted to be alone.

But there was soup and duckling, and red wine, dispensed by Eliot. The duckling was rich and the room very warm. As the meal slowly progressed I felt more and more strange, disembodied, light-headed. I tried to concentrate on the flames of the candles in front of me, but as I stared at them they separated and repeated themselves, and the voices around me became blurred and unintelligible, like the hum of conversation heard from a distant room. Instinctively, I pushed my plate away from me, knocked over the wineglass, and watched, in hopeless horror, as the red wine spread amongst the shattered splinters of glass.

In a way the accident was a blessing, for they all stopped talking and looked at me. I must have gone quite pale, for Eliot was on his feet in an instant and at my side . . .

"Are you all right?"

I said, "No, I don't think I am. I'm sorry . . ."

"Oh, my dear." Mollie flung aside her napkin and pushed back her chair. From across the table Andrea eyed me with chill interest.

"The glass . . . I'm so sorry . . ."

From the head of the table Grenville spoke. "It doesn't matter about the glass. Leave the glass. The girl's exhausted. Mollie, take her up and put her to bed."

I tried to protest, but not very hard. Eliot drew back my chair and helped me to my feet, his hands firm beneath my elbows. Mollie had gone to open the door, and cooler air moved in from the hall—already I felt better, as though, perhaps, after all I was not going to faint.

As I passed Grenville, I said, "I'm sorry," for the third time; "forgive me. Good night." I bent and kissed him, and left them all. Mollie closed the door behind us and came upstairs with me. She helped me undress and get into bed, and I was asleep before she had even turned off the light.

I slept for fourteen hours, waking at ten o'clock. I had not slept so late for years, and beyond my window the sky was blue and the cold bright northern light reflected from the sloping white-painted walls of my room. I got up, pulled on a dressing-gown and went and had a bath. Dressed, I felt wonderful, apart from the sinking sensation of shame at my behaviour the night before. I hoped they had not all thought that I was drunk.

Downstairs, I finally ran Mollie to earth in a little pantry, arranging a great mass of purple and pink polyanthus in a flowered bowl.

"How did you sleep?" she asked at once.

"Like the dead. I'm sorry about last night . . ."

"My dear, you were tired out. I'm sorry I didn't realize before. You'll want some breakfast."

"Just coffee."

She took me into the kitchen and heated coffee while I made some toast. "Where is everybody?" I asked.

"Eliot's at the garage, of course, and Pettifer's taken the car to Fourbourne to do some shopping for Grenville."

"What can I do? There must be something I can do to help."

"Well . . ." she debated. I looked at her. This morning she wore a cashmere sweater the colour of caramel and a slender tweed skirt. Immaculately made up, with every strand of hair in place, she seemed almost inhumanly neat. "You could go and fetch the fish for me in Porthkerris. The fishmonger rang up to say he'd got some halibut and I thought we'd have it for dinner. I could lend you my little car. Do you drive?"

"Yes, but couldn't I walk down? I like walking and it's such a lovely morning."

"Of course, if you want to. You could take the short cut over the fields and along the cliff. I know—" she appeared to be suddenly struck by inspiration—"take Andrea with you, and then she can show you the way, and show you where the fish shop is. Besides, she never takes any exercise if she can possibly help it and a walk would do her good." She made Andrea sound like a lazy dog. I did not particularly relish the idea of Andrea's company for the entire morning but I was sympathetic to Mollie, being encumbered by this unengaging girl, so I said that I would do as she suggested, and when I had finished my breakfast went in search of Andrea whom Mollie had last seen out on the terrace.

I found her bundled in a rug, lying on a long cane chair in a patch of sunshine, and peevishly regarding the view, like a seasick passenger on a liner.

"Will you walk down to Porthkerris with me?" I asked her.

She fixed me with her protuberant stare. "Why?"

"Because Mollie's asked me to go and pick up some fish and I don't know where the shop is. Besides, it's a lovely morning, and she thought we might go down to the cliffs."

She considered my suggestion, said, "All right," uncoiled herself from the rug and stood up. She wore the same dirty jeans as yesterday and a vast black and white sweater which reached below her narrow hips. We went back to the kitchen to fetch a basket and then set out, by way of the terrace and the sloping garden, down in the direction of the sea.

At the bottom of the garden, stone steps led up and over the wall, and Andrea went ahead of me, but I paused because I wanted to inspect the studio from this new angle. It was, as Joss had said, locked and shuttered, and somehow desolate, and the great window on the north wall had been closed off by tightly-drawn curtains so that not a chink presented itself to any inquisitive passer-by.

Andrea stood on the top of the wall, her gaze following mine.

"He never paints now," she told me.

"I know."

"I can't think why. There's nothing wrong with him." She jumped, hair flying, down off the wall, and totally disappeared. I took a last look at the studio and then followed her and we took a trodden path that led down through small, irregular fields, and came out at last, through the hazard of some waist-high gorse bushes, to a stile, and so on to the cliff path.

This was obviously a favourite walk with visitors to Porthkerris, for there were seats set in sheltered view points, and litter bins for rubbish, and notices warning people not to go too near the edge of the cliff which was likely to collapse.

Andrea instantly went to the very edge and

peered over. Gulls wheeled and screamed all around
her, the wind tore at her hair and the baggy sweater,
and from far below came the distant thunder of surf
on rocks. She flung her arms wide and teetered
slightly as though about to fall over the edge, but
when she saw that I didn't care whether she commit-
ted suicide or not, she returned to the path, and in
single file we walked on, Andrea in front.

The cliff curved and the town came into view in
front of us, the low grey houses nestled around the
sweep of the bay and climbing the steep hill to the
moor behind. We went through a gate, and were now
on to a proper road, and so able to walk side by side.

Andrea became conversational.

"Your mother's just died, hasn't she?"

"Yes."

"Aunt Mollie was telling me about her. She said
she was a tart."

Painfully, I remained serene. It would have been
instant victory for Andrea if I had been anything else.

"She didn't really know her. They hadn't seen
each other for years."

"Was she a tart?"

"No."

"Mollie said she lived with men."

I realized then that Andrea was not merely trying to needle me, she was genuinely curious, and
there was envy there as well.

I said, "She was very gay and very loving and
very beautiful."

She accepted this. "Where do you live?"

"In London. I've got a little flat."

"Do you live alone, or with somebody?"

"No, I live alone."

"Do you go to parties and things?"

"Yes, if someone asks me and I want to go."

"Do you work? Do you have a job?"

"Yes. In a bookshop."

"God, how grim."

"I like it."

"Where did you meet Joss?"

Now, I thought, we're getting down to business, but her face was empty of expression.

"I met him in London . . . he mended a chair for me."

"Do you like him?"

"I don't know him well enough to dislike him."

"Eliot hates him. So does Aunt Mollie."

"Why?"

"Because they don't like having him around the place all the time. And they treat him as though he should call them Sir and Madam, and of course he doesn't. And he talks to Grenville and makes him laugh. I've heard them talking."

I imagined her creeping up to closed doors, listening at keyholes.

"That's nice, if he makes the old man laugh."

"He and Eliot had a terrible row once. It was about some car that Eliot had sold to a friend of Joss's and Joss said it wasn't roadworthy and Eliot called him an insolent, interfering bastard."

"Did you listen in to that one as well?"

"I couldn't help hearing. I was in the loo and the window was open and they were out on the gravel by the front door."

"How long have you been staying at Boscarva?" I asked, curious to know how long it had taken her to dig all these skeletons out of the family cupboards.

"Two weeks. It seems like six months."

"I should have thought you'd have loved coming down."

"For heaven's sake, I'm not a child. What am I meant to do with myself. Go bucket and spading on the beach?"

"What do you do in London?"

She kicked a pebble, viciously, hating Cornwall. "I was at an art school, but my parents *didn't approve—*" she put on a mealy voice—"of my friends. So they took me away and sent me here."

"But you can't stay here for ever. What are you going to do when you go back?"

"That's up to them, isn't it?"

I felt a twinge of pity for her parents, even parents who had somehow raised such an obnoxious child.

"I mean, isn't there anything you *want* to do?"

"Yes, just get away, be on my own, do my own thing. Danus, this fabulous chap I went around with, he had a friend who was running a pottery on the Isle of Skye, and he wanted me to go and help . . . It sounded super, you know, living in a sort of commune, and right away from everybody . . . but my grotty mother shoved her great oar in and spoiled it all."

"Where's Danus now?"

"Oh, he went to Skye."

"Has he written to tell you about it?"

She tossed her head, fiddled with her hair, would not meet my eye. "Yes, actually, long letters. Reams of them. He still wants me to go there, and I'm going to, just as soon as I'm eighteen and they can't stop me any more."

"Why don't you go back to Art School first, and get some sort of a qualification . . . that'd give you time . . ."

She turned on me. "You know something? You talk like all the rest of them? How old are you anyway? You sound like someone with one foot in the grave."

"It's crazy to wreck your life before it's even started."

"It's my life. Not yours."

"No, it's not my life."

Having thus stupendously quarrelled, we continued our walk into the town in silence, and when Andrea did speak again, it was to say, "That's the fish shop," and wave a hand in its direction.

"Thank you." I went in to collect the halibut but she stayed, pointedly, outside on the cobbled pavement. When I emerged again, she had gone, only to appear the next moment from a papershop next door, where she had been buying a lurid magazine called *True Sex.*

"Shall we go back now?" I asked her. "Or do you want to do more shopping?"

"I can't shop, I haven't any money. Only a few pence."

I was suddenly, irrationally, sorry for her. "I'll stand you a cup of coffee if you'd like one."

She looked at me with sudden delight and I thought she was going to gleefully accept my modest offer, but instead she said, "Let's go and see Joss."

I was taken unawares. "Why do you want to go and see Joss?"

"I just do. I often go and see him when I come down to the town. He's always pleased to see me. He made me promise always to go and see him if I'm down here."

"How do you know he'll be there?"

"Well, he's not at Boscarva today, so he must be at the shop. Have you been there? It's super, he's got a sort of pad on the top floor, just like something out of a magazine, with a bed that's a sort of sofa and masses of cushions and things, and a log fire. And at night—" her voice became dreamy—"it's all closed-in and secret, and there's nothing but firelight."

I tried not to gape. "You mean . . . you and Joss . . ."

She shrugged, tossing her hair. "Once or twice, but nobody knows. I don't know why I told you. You won't tell the others, will you?"

"But don't they . . . doesn't Mollie . . . ask questions?"

"Oh, I tell her I'm going to the cinema. She doesn't seem to mind me going to the cinema. Come on, let's go and see Joss . . ."

But after this revelation, nothing would have induced me to go near Joss's shop. I said, "Joss will be working, he won't want to be interrupted. And anyway there isn't time. And I don't want to go."

"You said there was time for coffee, why isn't there time for Joss?"

"Andrea, I told you, I don't want to go."

She began to smile. "I thought you liked Joss."

"That's not the point. He doesn't want us under his feet every time he turns round."

"Do you mean me?"

"I mean *us.*" I was beginning to be desperate.

"He always wants to see me. I know he does."

"Yes, I'm sure," I said gently. "But let's go back to Boscarva."

I reminded myself that from the very start I had not liked Joss. Despite his concern and apparent friendliness he had always left me with that strange sensation of disquiet, as though someone were creeping up behind my back. Yesterday I had begun to forget this initial antipathy, even to like him, but after Andrea's confidences it was not hard to whip back to life my first distrust of the man. He was too good-looking, too charming. Andrea could be a liar, but she was no fool; she had pigeon-holed the rest of the family with disconcerting accuracy, and even if there

was only a grain of truth in what she said about Joss,
I wanted to have no part of it.

If I had known him and liked him better, I
would have taken him aside and taxed him with what
she had said. As it was, he held no importance for
me. Besides, I had other things to think about.

Grenville did not come down for lunch that day.

"He's tired," Mollie told us. "He's having a day
in bed. Perhaps he'll join us for dinner. Pettifer's going to take him up a tray."

So the three of us ate lunch together. Mollie had
changed into a neat woollen dress and a double string
of pearls. She was going, she said, to play bridge with
friends in Fourbourne. She hoped that I would be
able to occupy myself.

I said that of course I would be perfectly all
right. Across the table, we smiled at each other and I
wondered if she had really told Andrea that my
mother was a tart, or if this was simply Andrea's
interpretation of some vague euphemistic explanation
that Mollie had given her. I hoped it was the latter,
but still I wished that Mollie had not found it neces-
sary to discuss Lisa with Andrea. She was dead now,
but once she had been funny and enchanting and full
of laughter. Why couldn't she be remembered that
way?

As we sat around the table, the day outside
changed its face. A wind got up from the west, and
with great speed a bank of grey cloud sped over the
blue sky, obliterating the sunshine, and presently it

started to rain. It was in this rain that Mollie set off for her bridge party, driving her little car, and saying that she would be home about six. Andrea, perhaps exhausted by her morning's exercise, but more likely bored to death with my company, disappeared up to her bedroom with her new magazine. Alone, I stood at the foot of the stairs, wondering how to amuse myself. The silence of the gloomy afternoon was broken only by the ticking of the grandfather clock and small, occupied sounds which came from the direction of the kitchens, and which, investigated, proved to be Pettifer, seated at a wooden table in his pantry and cleaning silver.

He looked up as I put my head around the door.

"Hallo. I didn't hear you."

"How's my grandfather?"

"Oh, he's all right. Just a bit weary after all the excitement of yesterday. We thought it would be better if he had a day with his toes up. Has Mrs Roger gone?"

"Yes." I pulled up a chair and sat opposite him.

"Thought I heard the car."

"Do you want me to help you?"

"That'd be very kind . . . those spoons there need a good rub up with the shammy. Don't know how they get so marked and stained. But, there, I do know. It's this damp sea air. One thing silver really hates it's damp sea air." I began to rub at the thin worn bowl of the spoon. Pettifer looked at me over the top of his glasses. "Funny to have you sitting there after all these years. Your mother used to spend half her life in the kitchen . . . When Roger went off to boarding school there wasn't anyone else for her to talk to. So she used to come and spend her time with Mrs Pettifer and me. Taught her to make Fairy Cakes, Mrs Pettifer did, and how to play two-handed whist. We had great times. And on a day like this, she used to make toast at the old range . . . mind, that's gone now, we've got a new one and good thing too . . . but that old range was cosy, with the fire burning behind the bars, and all the brass knobs polished up lovely."

"How long have you been at Boscarva, Pettifer?"

"Ever since the Commander bought it, back in 1922. That was the year he left the Navy, decided to be a painter. Old Mrs Bayliss didn't like that. For three months or more she wouldn't even talk to him."

"Why did she mind so much?"

"She'd been with the Navy all her life. Her father was the Captain of the *Imperious* when the Commander was First Lieutenant. That was how they met. They were married in Malta. A lovely wedding with an arch of swords and all. Being with the Navy meant a lot to Mrs Bayliss. When the Commander said he was going to leave they parted brass rags good and proper, but she couldn't make him change his mind. So we left Malta, for good and all, and the Commander found this house, and then we all moved down here."

"And you've been here ever since?"

"More or less. The Commander enrolled at the Slade, and that meant working in London, so he had this little *pied-à-terre,* just off St James's it was, and when he went up to London I went too, to keep an eye on him, and Mrs Pettifer stayed here with Mrs Bayliss and Roger. Your mother wasn't born then."

"But, when he'd finished at the Slade . . . ?"

"Well, then he came back for good. And built the studio. That was when he was painting at his best. Lovely stuff he did then, great seascapes, so cold and bright you could smell the wind, feel the salt on your lips."

"Are there many of his pictures in this house?"

"No, not many. There's the fishing boat over the dining-room fireplace, and one or two little black and white drawings along the upstairs passage. He's got three or four in his study, and then there's a couple in the room where Mrs Roger sleeps."

"And the one in the drawing room . . ."

"Oh, yes, that one of course. 'Lady Holding a Rose.' "

"Who was she?"

He did not reply; was, perhaps, preoccupied with his silver, rubbing away at a fork as though determined to flatten the pattern.

"Who was she? The girl in the picture?"

"Oh," said Pettifer. "That was Sophia."

Sophia. Ever since my mother had fleetingly mentioned her I had wanted to know about Sophia, and now here was Pettifer bringing up her name as though it were the most natural thing in the world.

"She was a girl who used to model for the Commander. I think she first worked for him in London when he was a student, and then she used to come down here sometimes during the summer months, take lodgings in Porthkerris and work for any artist who was ready and able to pay her."

"Was she very beautiful?"

"Not my idea of a beauty. But lively, and what a talker! She was Irish, she'd come from County Cork."

"What did my grandmother think of Sophia?"

"Their paths never crossed, any more than your grandmother would have had social dealings with the butcher or the girl who did her hair."

"So Sophia never came to Boscarva?"

"Oh, yes, she used to come and go. She'd be down at the studio with the Commander, and then he'd get tired, or lose his patience with her, and call it a day, and she'd come up the garden and through the back door calling out, 'Any chance of a cup of tea?' and because it was Sophia, Mrs Pettifer always had the kettle on."

"She used to tell fortunes from teacups."

"Who told you that?"

"My mother."

"That's right, she did. And wonderful things she told us were going to happen to us all. 'Course, they didn't, but it was fun listening to her, just the same. She and your mother were great friends. Sophia used to take her down to the beach and Mrs Pettifer would pack a picnic. And if it was stormy weather they'd go long walks up on the moor."

"But what was my grandmother doing all this time?"

"Oh, playing bridge or mah-jongg most afternoons. She had a very select circle of friends. She was a nice enough lady, but not really interested in children. Perhaps if she'd been more interested in Lisa when she was a child, they'd have had more in common when Lisa grew up, and maybe your mother wouldn't have run off like that, breaking all our hearts."

"What happened to Sophia?"

"Oh, she went back to London, she got married and she had a baby, I think. Then, in 1942, she was killed in the Blitz. The baby was down in the country and her husband was overseas, but Sophia stayed in London because she was working in a hospital there. We didn't hear about it for a long time, till long after it happened. Mrs Pettifer and I felt as though a light had gone out of our lives."

"And my grandfather?"

"He was sorry, of course. But he hadn't seen her for years. She was just a girl who'd once worked for him."

"Are there any more pictures of her?"

"There's pictures of Sophia in provincial art galleries up and down the country. There's one in the gallery in Porthkerris if you want to go and look at that. And there's a couple upstairs in Mrs Roger's bedroom."

"Could we go and look at them now?" I sounded eager and Pettifer looked surprised, as though I were suggesting something faintly indecent. "I mean Mrs Bayliss wouldn't mind, would she?"

"Oh, she wouldn't mind. I don't see why not . . . come on."

He got laboriously to his feet, and I followed him upstairs and along the first-floor passage to the bedroom over the drawing room, which was large and furnished in a very feminine fashion with old-fashioned Victorian furniture and a faded pink and cream carpet. Mollie had left it painfully neat. The two little oil paintings hung side by side between the windows, one of a chestnut tree with a girl lying in its shade, the other of the same girl hanging out a line of washing on a breezy day. They were scarcely more than sketches, and I was disappointed.

"I still don't know what Sophia looks like."

Pettifer was about to reply when, from the depths of the house, came the ringing of a bell. He cocked his head, like a dog listening. "That's the Commander, he's heard us talking through the wall. Excuse me a moment."

I followed him out of Mollie's room and closed the door behind me. He went on down the passage a little way and opened a door, and I heard Grenville's voice.

"What are you two muttering about in there?"

"I was just showing Rebecca the two pictures in Mrs Roger's room . . ."

"Is Rebecca there? Tell her to come in . . ."

I went in, past Pettifer. Grenville was not in bed, but sitting in a deep arm-chair with his feet propped up on a stool. He was dressed, but there was a rug over his knees and the room was cheered by the flicker of a fire. Everything was very neat and ship-shape and smelt of the Bay Rum he put on his hair.

I said, "I thought you were in bed."

"Pettifer got me up after lunch. I get bored stiff lying in bed all day. What have you been talking about?"

"Pettifer was showing me some of your pictures."

"I expect you think they're very old-fashioned. They're going back to realism now, you know, these young artists. I knew it would come. You'll have to have one of my pictures. There are racks of them in the studio that have never been sorted out. I closed the place up ten years ago, and I haven't been there since. Pettifer, where's the key?"

"Put safely away, sir."

"You'll have to get the key off Pettifer, go down and nose around, see if there's anything you'd like. Got anywhere to hang it?"

"I've got a flat in London. It needs a picture."

"I thought of something else sitting here. That jade in the cabinet downstairs. I brought it back from China years ago, gave it to Lisa. Now, it belongs to you. And a mirror that her grandmother left her—where's that, Pettifer?"

"That's in the morning room, sir."

"Well, we'll have to get it down, give it a clean. You'd like that, wouldn't you?"

"Yes, I would." I felt greatly relieved. I had been wondering how to bring up the subject of my mother's possessions, and now, without any prompting, Grenville had done it for me. I hesitated and then, striking while the iron was hot, mentioned the third thing. ". . . and there was a davenport desk."

"Hm?" He fixed me with his ferocious stare. "How do you know?"

"My mother told me about the jade and the mirror, and she said there was a davenport desk." He continued to glare at me. I wished all at once that I had said nothing. "I mean, it doesn't matter, it's just that if nobody did want it . . . if it wasn't being used . . ."

"Pettifer, do you remember that desk?"

"Yes, I do, sir, now you come to mention it. It was up in the other attic bedroom, but I can't remember having seen it lately."

"Well, look for it some time, there's a good fellow. And put another bit of wood on the fire . . ." Pettifer did so. Grenville, watching him, said suddenly, "Where is everybody? The house is quiet. Only the sound of the rain."

"Mrs Roger's out to a bridge party. I think Miss Andrea's in her room . . ."

"How about a cup of tea?" Grenville cocked an eye at me. "You'd like a cup of tea, wouldn't you? We haven't had the chance of getting to know each other. Either you're keeling over in the middle of dinner, or

I'm too old and infirm to get out of bed. We make a
fine pair, don't we?"

"I'd like to have tea with you."

"Pettifer will bring up a tray."

"No," I said. "I will. Pettifer's legs have been up
and down these stairs all day. Let's give him a rest."

Grenville looked amused. "All right. You bring
it up, and let's have a good big plateful of hot buttered toast."

I was to wish, many times over, that I had never
brought up the subject of the davenport desk. Because it could not be found. While Grenville and I ate
our tea, Pettifer began to look for it. By the time he
came to take the tray away, he had combed the house
from top to bottom, and the desk was nowhere.

Grenville scarcely believed him. "You've just
missed it. Your eyes are getting as old as mine."

"I could scarcely miss seeing a desk." Pettifer
sounded aggrieved.

"Perhaps," I said, trying to be helpful, "it was
sent away to be mended or something . . ." They
both looked at me as though I were a fool, and I
hastily shut up.

"Would it be in the studio?" Pettifer ventured.

"What would I do with a desk in the studio? I
painted there, I didn't write letters. Didn't want a
desk cluttering the place up . . ." Grenville was getting quite agitated. I stood up, "Oh, it'll turn up," I
said in my best, soothing voice, and picked up the tea
tray to carry it downstairs. In the kitchen I was
joined by Pettifer, upset by what had happened.

"It's not good for the Commander to get worked up about anything . . . and he's going to go after this like a terrier after a rat. I can tell."

"It's all my fault. I don't know why I even mentioned it."

"But I remember it. I just can't remember having seen it lately." I began to wash the cups and saucers and Pettifer picked up a tea towel in order to dry them. "And there's another thing. There was a Chippendale chair that used to go with it . . . mind, they didn't match, but the chair always sat in front of that desk. It had a tapestry seat, rather worn, birds and flowers and things. Well, that's gone, too . . . but I'm not going to tell the Commander that and neither are you."

I promised that I wouldn't. "Anyway," I said, "it doesn't matter to me one way or the other."

"No, but it matters to the Commander. Artistic he may have been, but he had a memory like an elephant and that's one thing he hasn't lost." He added gloomily, "I sometimes wish he had."

That evening when I went downstairs, changed once more into the brown and silver caftan, I found Eliot in the drawing room, alone except for that inevitable companion, his dog. Eliot sat by the fire with a drink and the evening paper, and Rufus was stretched, like some glorious fur, on the hearthrug. They looked companionable, caught in the light of the lamp, but my appearance disturbed the peaceful scene, and Eliot stood up, dropping the paper behind him on the seat of the chair.

"Rebecca. How are you?"

"I'm all right."

"I was afraid last night that you were going to be ill."

"No. I was just tired. I slept till ten o'clock."

"My mother told me. Would you like a drink?"

I said that I would and he poured me some sherry and I went to crouch by the fire and fondle the dog's silky ears.

As Eliot brought me my drink I asked, "Does he go everywhere with you?"

"Yes, everywhere. To the garage, to the office, out to lunch, into the pubs, anywhere I happen to be going. He's a very well-known dog in this part of the world."

I sat on the hearthrug, and Eliot subsided once more into his chair and picked up his drink. He said, "Tomorrow I have to go over to Falmouth, see a man about a car. I wondered if you'd like to come with me, see a bit of the country. Does that appeal to you?"

I was surprised by my own pleasure at this invitation. "I'd love it."

"It won't be very exciting. But perhaps you can amuse yourself for an hour or two while I'm doing business, and then we'll stop at a little pub I know on the way home. They serve delicious sea food. Do you like oysters?"

"Yes."

"Good. So do I. And then we'll come home by

High Cross, and you can see where we normally live, my mother and I."

"Your mother told me about it. It sounds charming."

"Better than this mausoleum . . ."

"Oh, Eliot, it's not a mausoleum . . ."

"I was never much of a one for Victorian relics . . ."

Before I could protest further, we were joined by Grenville. At least, we heard him coming, step by step downstairs; heard him talking to Pettifer, the high-pitched voice and the low growl; heard them coming down the hall, the tap of Grenville's stick on the polished wood.

Eliot made a small face at me and went to open the door, and Grenville moved in, like the prow of some great, indestructible ship . . .

"That's all right, Pettifer, I can manage now." I had got up from the hearthrug, wanting to help push forward the chair which he had used the night before, but this seemed to madden him. He was obviously not in a good mood.

"For God's sake, girl, stop fussing around. Do you think I want to sit *in* the fire, I'll burn to death sitting there . . ."

I edged the chair back to its original position and finally Grenville reached it and sank into it.

"How about a drink?" Eliot asked him.

"I'll have a whisky . . ."

Eliot looked surprised . . . "Whisky?"

"Yes, a whisky. I know what that fool of a doctor said but tonight I'm having a whisky."

Eliot said nothing, just nodded his head in patient acquiescence and went to pour the drink. As he did so Grenville leaned round the edge of the chair and said, "Eliot, have you seen that davenport desk around the place?" and my heart sank into my shoes.

"Oh, Grenville, don't start that again . . ."

"What do you mean, start that again? We've got to find the damned thing. I told Pettifer just now, got to go on looking till we've found it."

Eliot came back with the glass of whisky. He drew up a table and set the glass within Grenville's reach.

"What davenport desk?" he asked patiently.

"Little davenport desk, used to be in one of the bedrooms. Belonged to Lisa, and now it belongs to Rebecca. She wants it. She's got a flat in London, wants to put it there. And Pettifer can't find it, says he's been through the house with a toothcomb, can't find it. You haven't seen it, have you?"

"I've never set eyes on it. I don't even know what a davenport desk is."

"It's a little desk. Got drawers down the side. Bit of tooled leather on the top. They're rare now, I believe. Worth a lot of money."

"Pettifer's probably put it somewhere and forgotten."

"Pettifer doesn't forget things."

"Well, perhaps Mrs Pettifer did something with it and forgot to tell him."

"I've already *said;* he doesn't forget things."

We were joined at this moment by Mollie, who appeared, smiling determinedly, as though she had heard the angry voice raised beyond the closed door, and was about to spread oil on troubled waters.

"Hallo, everybody, I'm afraid I'm a little late. I had to go and do some very exciting things to that delicious piece of halibut Rebecca bought for me this morning. Eliot, dear . . ." she kissed him, apparently seeing him for the first time that evening. "And Grenville—" she stooped to kiss him too—"you're looking more rested." Then, before he could contradict her, she smiled across the top of his head at me. "Did you have a good afternoon?"

"Yes, thank you. How was the bridge?"

"Not too bad. I won twenty pence. Eliot darling, I'd love a drink. Andrea's just coming. She won't be a moment . . ." But she finally ran out of defensive small talk, and Grenville instantly opened fire. "We've lost something," he told her.

"What have you lost? Your cuff-links again?"

"We have lost a davenport desk."

It was becoming ludicrous.

"You've *lost* a davenport desk?"

For her benefit, Grenville went through the whole rigmarole. On being told that it was I who had precipitated this crisis, Mollie looked at me with some reproach, as though she thought this a poor way to return her hospitality and kindness. I was inclined to agree with her.

"But it must be somewhere." She took her glass

from Eliot, drew up a stool and sat, all ready to work the whole thing out. "It must have been put somewhere for safety."

"Pettifer has looked for it."

"Perhaps he hasn't seen it. I'm sure he should get his glasses changed. Perhaps it's been put somewhere and he's forgotten."

Grenville thumped the arm of his chair with a balled fist. "Pettifer does not forget things."

"In fact—" said Eliot coolly—"he forgets things all the time."

Grenville glared at him. "And what does that mean?"

"Nothing personal. Just that he's getting older."

"I suppose you're blaming Pettifer . . ."

"I'm not blaming anybody . . ."

"You just said he's too old to know what he's doing. If he's too old what the hell do you think I am?"

"I never said that . . ."

"You blamed *him* . . ."

Eliot lost his patience. "If I was going to blame anybody," he said, raising his voice almost to the pitch of Grenville's, "I'd ask a few questions of young Joss Gardner." There was a pause after he'd come out with this. And then, in a more controlled, reasonable voice, he went on. "All right, so nobody wants to accuse another man of stealing. But Joss is in and out of this house all the time, in and out of all the rooms. He knows what's in this place better than anybody. And he's an expert, he knows what it's worth."

"But why should Joss take a desk?" asked Mollie.

"A valuable desk. Don't forget that. It's rare and it's valuable, Grenville just said so. Perhaps he needed the money. To look at him he could do with a bit of extra cash. And he's an expert. He's up and down to London all the time. He'd know where to sell it."

He stopped, abruptly, as though realizing that already he had said too much. He finished his whisky, and went, without speaking, to pour himself a second glass.

The silence became uncomfortable. To break it, Mollie said, briefly, "I don't think that Joss . . ."

"Just a lot of poppycock," Grenville interrupted her savagely.

Eliot set down the whisky bottle with a thump. "How do you know? How do you know anything about Joss Gardner? He turns up, like a hippy, out of nowhere, says he's going to open a shop, and the next thing you've opened up the house to him and given him the job of patching up all the furniture. What do you know about Joss? What do any of us know about him?"

"I know that I can trust him. I was trained to judge a man's character . . ."

"You could be wrong . . ."

Grenville raised his voice and rode over Eliot's, ". . . and it would be no bad thing if you were to take a few lessons in choosing your companions."

Eliot's eyes narrowed. "What does that mean?"

"It means that if you want to be made a fool of, try doing business with that little shyster Ernest Padlow."

If I could have escaped at that moment, I would. But I was caught, jammed into the corner behind Grenville's chair.

"What do you know about Ernest Padlow?"

"I know you've been seen around with him . . . drinking in bars . . ."

Eliot shot a glance at me, and then said, under his breath, "That bastard Joss Gardner."

"It wasn't Joss who told me, it was Hargreaves, at the bank. He came up for a glass of sherry the other day. And Mrs Thomas came in to do my fire this morning, she'd seen you with Padlow, up at that gimcrack nightmare he calls a housing estate."

"Back-stairs gossip."

"You hear the truth from truthful people. It doesn't matter in which direction they live. And if you think I'm selling up my land to that jumped-up little beachsweeper, you're wrong . . ."

"It won't always be your land."

"And if you're so sure it will be yours, all I can say is, don't count your chickens before they're hatched. Because you, dear boy, are not my only grandchild."

And at this dramatic moment, like a nicely stage-managed play, the door opened and Andrea appeared to tell us that Pettifer had told her to tell us that dinner was ready.

8

It was hard to sleep that night. I tossed and turned, fetched a glass of water, paced the floor, looked out of the window, climbed back into bed and tried once more to compose myself, but always, when I closed my eyes, the evening came back to me like a film played over and over, voices drummed in my ears, and would not be stilled.

All right, so nobody wants to accuse another man of stealing. What do any of us know about Joss?

If you want to be made a fool of, try doing business with that little shyster Ernest Padlow. And if you think I'm selling my land to that jumped-up little beachsweeper, you're wrong . . .

It won't always be your land . . .

. . . you, dear boy, are not my only grandchild.

Dinner had been a gruesome meal. Eliot and Grenville had scarcely spoken a word from beginning to end. Mollie, to make up for their silence, had kept up a patter of meaningless conversation to which I had tried to respond. And Andrea had watched us all, a gleam of triumph in her round, seeking eyes, while Pettifer trod heavily to and fro, removing dishes, handing round a lemon soufflé rich with whipped cream, which nobody seemed to want.

When at last it was over, they had all dispersed. Grenville to his bedroom, Andrea to the morning room from whence we presently heard the blare of the television set. Eliot, with no explanations, put on a coat, whistled up his dog and banged out of the front door. I guessed he had gone to get drunk and didn't entirely blame him. Mollie and I ended up in the drawing room, one on either side of the fire. She had some tapestry and seemed quite prepared to sit and sew in silence, but this would have been unbearable. I said, plunging straight in with the apology which I felt I owed her, "I am sorry about this evening. I wish I'd never mentioned that desk."

She did not look at me. "Oh, it can't be helped."

"It was just that my mother had mentioned it to me, and when Grenville spoke about the jade and the mirror, well, it never occurred to me that I'd start such a storm in a tea-cup."

"Grenville's a strange old man. He's always been stubborn about people, he'll never see that there can be two sides to every situation."

"You mean about Joss . . ."

"I don't know why he's so taken with Joss. It's frightening. It's as though Joss were able to exert some hold over him. Eliot and I never wanted him in and out of the house this way. If Grenville's furniture needed to be repaired, surely he could have come and fetched it in his van and taken it down to his workshop, like any other tradesman would do. We tried to talk Grenville out of it, but he was adamant, and, after all, this is his house. It isn't ours."

"But it will be Eliot's one day."

She sent me a cold look.

"After this evening, one wonders."

"Oh, Mollie, I don't want Boscarva, Grenville would never leave a place like this to me. He just said that to win a point; perhaps it was the first thing that came into his head. He didn't mean it."

"He hurt Eliot."

"Eliot will understand. You have to make allowances for old people."

"I'm tired of making allowances for Grenville," said Mollie, viciously snapping at a strand of wool with her silver scissors. "My life has been disrupted by Grenville. He and Pettifer could have come and lived at High Cross; that's what we wanted. The house is smaller and more convenient and it would have been better for everybody. And Boscarva should have been made over to Eliot years ago. As it is, death duties are going to be exorbitant. Eliot is never going to be able to afford to keep it going. The whole situation is *so* unrealistic."

"I suppose it's hard to be realistic when you're eighty and you've lived in a place most of your life."

She ignored this. "And all that land, and the farm. Eliot is simply trying to make the best of it all, but Grenville won't see that. He's never shown any interest, never encouraged Eliot in any way. Even the garage at High Cross, Eliot got that going entirely on his own. At the beginning, he asked his grandfather to help, but Grenville said he wasn't going to have anything to do with second-hand cars, and there was a row, and finally Eliot borrowed the money from someone else, and he's never asked his grandfather for a shilling since that day. You'd think he'd deserve some credit for that."

She was pale with anger on Eliot's account—a little tigress, I thought, fighting for her cub, and I remembered my mother's low opinion of the way in which she had possessed and molly-coddled the young Eliot. Perhaps neither of them had ever grown out of the habit.

To change the subject I told her about Eliot's invitation for the next day. "He said he'd take me into High Cross on the way home."

But Mollie was only momentarily diverted. "You must go in and see the house, Eliot's got the key. I go up most weeks to make sure everything's all right, but really I get so depressed having to leave my darling little house and come back to this gloomy place . . ." and then she laughed at herself wryly. "It's getting me down, isn't it? I must try to pull myself together. But really I'll be glad when it's all over."

When it's all over. That meant when Grenville finally died. I didn't want to think about him dying any more than I wanted to think about Joss coupled with the unsavoury Andrea; any more than I wanted to think about Joss helping himself to a davenport desk and a Chippendale chair, heaving them into the back of his little truck, and selling them to the first dealer who made him a good offer.

What do you know about Joss? What do any of us know about him?

For my part I wished I knew nothing. I turned in bed, thumped at the pillows, and waited, without much hope, for sleep.

It rained in the night, but the next morning it was still and clear, the sky a pale, washed blue, everything wet and shining, translucent in the cool spring light. I leaned out of the window and smelt the dampness, mossy and sweet. The sea was flat and blue as a sheet of silk, gulls drifted lazily over the rim of the cliff, a boat moved out from the harbour, heading for distant fishing-grounds, and so still was the air that I could hear the distant chug of its engine.

My spirits rose. Yesterday was over, today would be better. I was glad to be getting out of the house, away from Mollie's reproach and Andrea's unsettling presence. I bathed and dressed and went downstairs and found Eliot in the dining room, eating bacon and eggs, and looking—I was thankful to see—cheerful.

He looked up from the morning paper. "I wondered," he said, "if I was going to have to come and wake you up. I thought perhaps you'd forgotten."

"No, I didn't forget."

"We're the first down. With any luck we'll be out of the house before anyone else appears." He grinned, ruefully, like a repentant boy. "The last thing I want on a beautiful morning like this is re-criminations."

"It was all my fault, mentioning that stupid desk. I said I was sorry last night to your mother."

"It'll all blow over," said Eliot. "These little differences of opinion always do." I poured myself a cup of coffee. "I'm just sorry that you were involved."

We left straight after breakfast, and there was a marvellous feeling of relief to be in his car, with Rufus perched on the back seat, and to be escaping. The car roared up the hill away from Boscarva; the wet road was blue with reflected sky, and the air smelt of primroses. As we climbed up and over the moor, the view spread and dipped before us—there were hills topped by ancient cairns and standing stones, and tiny forgotten villages, tucked into the folds of unexpected valleys where little rivers ran, and ancient clumps of oak and elm stood clustered by narrow, hump-backed bridges.

But I knew that we could not enjoy our day together, that we could not be entirely at ease, until I had made my peace with him.

I said, "I know that it'll blow over, and that perhaps it *wasn't* important, but we have to talk about last night."

He smiled at me, glancing sideways. "What do we have to say?"

"Just that, what Grenville said about having another grandchild. He didn't mean it. I know he didn't mean it."

"No, perhaps he didn't. Perhaps he was just trying to set us against each other, like a pair of dogs."

"He'd never leave me Boscarva. Never in a thousand years. He doesn't even know me, I've only just come into his life."

"Rebecca, don't give it another thought. I'm not going to."

"And, after all, if it is going to be yours one day, I don't see why you shouldn't start thinking about what you're going to do with it."

"You mean Ernest Padlow? What a lot of gossips those old people are, carrying tales and making mischief. If it isn't the bank manager it's Mrs Thomas, and if it isn't Mrs Thomas it's Pettifer."

I made myself sound casual. "Would you sell the land?"

"If I did, I could probably afford to live at Boscarva. It's time I set up on my own."

"But—" I chose my words tactfully—"but wouldn't it be rather . . . spoiled . . . I mean, living there with rows of Mr Padlow's little houses all round you?"

Eliot laughed. "You've got entirely the wrong end of the stick. This wouldn't be a building estate like the one at the top of the hill. This would be high-class stuff, two acre lots, very high specifications as to the style and the price of the houses built on them. No cutting down of trees, no despoiling of the amenities. They'd be expensive houses for expensive people, and there wouldn't be a lot of them. How does that sound to you?"

"Have you told Grenville this?"

"He won't let me. He won't listen. He's not interested and that's it."

"But surely if you explained . . ."

"I've been trying to explain things to him all my life and I've never got anywhere. And now, is there anything else you want to discuss?"

I considered. I certainly didn't want to discuss Joss. I said, "No."

"In that case shall we forget about last night and enjoy ourselves?"

It seemed a good idea. We smiled at each other. "All right," I said at last. We crossed a bridge and came to a steep hill, and Eliot changed down, expertly, with the old-fashioned gear stick. The car poured up the savage slope, its long, elegant bonnet seeming to point straight to the sky.

We got to Falmouth about ten o'clock. While Eliot attended to his business I was turned loose to explore the little town. Facing south, sheltered from the north wind, with gardens already filled with camellias and scented daphne bushes, it made me think of some Mediterranean port, and this illusion was strengthened by the blue of the sea on that first warm spring day, and the tall masts of the yachts which lay at anchor in the basin.

I felt, for some reason, impelled to shop. I bought freesias for Mollie, tightly in bud with their stalks wrapped in damp moss so that they would not wither before I got home, a box of cigars for Grenville, a bottle of fruity sherry for Pettifer, a record for

Andrea. The sleeve portrayed a transvestite group
with sequined eyelids. It seemed to me to be right up
her street. And for Eliot . . . I had noticed that his
watch strap was wearing thin. I found a narrow strap
in dark crocodile, very expensive, exactly right for
Eliot. Then I bought a tube of toothpaste for myself,
because I needed one. And for Joss . . . ? Nothing
for Joss.

Eliot picked me up, as we had arranged, in the
lounge of the big hotel in the middle of town. We
drove very fast out of the town and through Truro,
and down into the little maze of lanes and wooded
creeks that lay beyond until we came to a village
called St Endon, where there were white cottages,
palm trees and gardens full of flowers. The road
wound down towards the creek, and at the very bottom was a little pub, right on the water's edge, with
the high tide lapping at the wall below the terrace.
Kittiwakes perched along the top of it, their eyes
bright and friendly, unlike the greedy, wild gulls of
Boscarva.

We sat out in the sunshine, drinking sherry, and
I gave Eliot his present, then and there; he seemed
inordinately delighted, ripping off the old watch strap
right away and fitting on the new, shining leather
one, adjusting the little clips with the blade of his
penknife.

"What made you think of giving me that?"

"I noticed your old one was worn. I thought
perhaps that you might lose your watch."

He leaned back in his chair, watching me across

the table. It was so warm that I had pulled off my sweater and rolled up the sleeves of my cotton shirt. He said, "Did you buy presents for everybody?"

I was embarrassed. "Yes."

"I thought you had a lot of parcels. Do you always buy presents for people?"

"It's nice to have people to buy presents for."

"Isn't there anyone in London?"

"Not really."

"No one special?"

"There's never been anyone special."

"I can't believe it."

"It's true." I could not think why I was confiding in him this way. Perhaps it had something to do with the warmth of the day, surprising me by its beneficence, lowering all my guards. Perhaps it was the sherry. Perhaps it was simply the intimacy of two people who had weathered such a storm as the row that had taken place last night. Whatever the reason, it was easy that day to talk to Eliot.

"Why is that?" he asked.

"I don't know. It may have something to do with the way I was brought up . . . my mother lived with one man after another, so I lived with them too. And there's nothing like living at close quarters with people to destroy that marvellous illusion of romance."

We laughed. "That could be a good thing," said Eliot. "But it could be a bad thing, too. You mustn't close up altogether. Otherwise nobody's ever going to get near you."

"I'm all right."

"Are you going back to London?"

"Yes."

"Soon?"

"Probably."

"Why not stay for a bit?"

"I don't want to wear out my welcome."

"You won't do that. And I've hardly spoken to you. Anyway, how can you go back to London and leave all this behind you . . . ?" His gesture included the sky, the sun, the quiet, the lap of water, the promise of the coming spring.

"I can, because I have to. I've a job to get back to and a flat that needs painting, and a life to pick up and start all over again."

"Can't that wait?"

"Not indefinitely."

"There's no reason to go." I did not reply. "Unless," he went on, "you were put off by what happened last night." I smiled and shook my head, because we had promised not to mention that again. He leaned on the table, his chin on his fist. "If you really wanted a job you could get one here. If you wanted a flat of your own you could rent that too."

"Why should I stay?" But I was flattered at being so persuaded.

"Because it would be good for Grenville, and for Mollie, and for me. Because I think we all want you to stay. Particularly me."

"Oh, Eliot . . ."

"It's true. There's something very serene about

you. Did you know that? I noticed it that first evening I saw you before I even knew who you were.
And I like the shape of your nose, and the sound of
your laugh, and the way you can look marvellously
ragamuffin one minute, in jeans and with your hair
coming all unravelled, and then, the next minute, like
a princess in a fairy story, with your plait over your
shoulder and that stately gown you wear in the evenings. I feel as though I'm finding out new things
about you every day. And this is why I don't want
you to go. Not just yet."

I found that I could think of no rejoinder to this
long speech. I was touched by it, and embarrassed
too. But still, it was gratifying to be liked and ad-
mired, and even more gratifying to be told so.

Across the table, he began to laugh at me. "Your
face is a picture. You don't know where to look and
you're blushing. Come along, finish your drink and
we'll go and eat oysters—I promise I'll not pay you
any more compliments!"

We lingered over lunch in the small, low-ceilinged dining room, eating at a table which wobbled
so much on the uneven floor that Eliot was forced to
prop up one of the legs with a scrap of folded paper.
We ate oysters and steak and a fresh green salad and
drank our way through a bottle of wine. We took our
coffee back into the sunshine, and sat on the edge of
the terrace wall, watching two boys, sunburned and
barelegged, rig up a dinghy and take her sailing out
on to the blue waters of the creek. We saw the striped
sail fill with some mysterious, unfelt breeze, as the

dinghy heeled and went away from us, around the tip of a wooded promontory. And Eliot said that if I stayed in Cornwall, he would borrow a boat and teach me to sail; we would go mackerel fishing from Porthkerris—in the summer he would show me all the tiny coves and secret places which the tourists never found.

At last it was time to go, and the afternoon wound itself in like a long, shining ribbon. Sleepy and replete he drove me slowly back to High Cross, taking the long road that led through forgotten villages and the heart of the country.

When we got to High Cross, I realized that it stood at the very summit of the peninsula, so that the village had two aspects, one north to the Atlantic, the other south to the Channel; it was like being on an island, swept with clean winds and ringed by the sea. Eliot's garage stood in the middle of the village street, a little back from the road, with a cobbled forecourt set about with tubs of flowers, and inside the glass-fronted showroom stood the gleaming, racy cars. Everything was very new and expensive looking and immaculately kept. I wondered, as we crossed the forecourt towards the showrooms, how much Eliot had had to sink into such a venture, and why he had decided that it was a viable proposition to open such a specialized garage in this out-of-the-way spot.

He pulled one of the sliding glass doors aside and I went in, my feet making no sound on the highly polished rubber floors.

"Why did you decide to start your garage here,

Eliot? Wouldn't it have been better in Fourbourne or Falmouth or Penzance?"

"Psychological selling, my dear. Get a good name for yourself and people will come from the ends of the earth to buy what you've got to sell." And he added with disarming candour, "Besides, I already owned the land, or at least my mother did, which was an excellent incentive to build the garage here."

"Are all these cars for sale?"

"Yes. As you can see we concentrate on continental and sports cars. We had a Ferrari in last week, but that was sold a couple of days ago. It had been crashed, but I've got this young mechanic working for me, and by the time he'd finished with it it was as good as new . . ."

I laid my hand on the gleaming yellow bonnet. "What's this?"

"A Lancia Zagato. And this is an Alfa Romeo Spyder, only two years old. Beautiful car."

"And a Jensen Interceptor . . ." That was one that I recognized.

"Come and see the workshop." I followed him through another sliding door at the back of the showroom and decided that this was more like my idea of a garage. Here was the usual clutter of dismantled engines, oil cans, long flexes trailing from the ceiling, naked bulbs, tool benches, old tyres and trolleys.

In the middle of all this a figure was stooped over the stripped-down engine of a skeletal car. He wore a welding mask which made him appear monstrous, and worked with the roaring blue flame of a welding gun. The noise of the gun was overlaid by non-stop blaring music from a surprisingly small transistor radio perched on a beam above him.

Whether or not he saw us coming was anybody's guess, but it was only when Eliot switched off the radio that he shut off his gun and straightened up, pushing the welding mask up and back off his face. I saw a thin, dark young man, oil-stained and in need of a shave, his hair long, his eyes sharp and bright.

"Hallo, Morris," said Eliot.

"Hallo."

"This is Rebecca Bayliss, she's staying at Boscarva."

Reaching for a cigarette, Morris looked my way and gave me a nod. I said, "Hallo," just to be friendly, but got no more response. He lit his cigarette, then slipped the fancy lighter back into the pocket of his oily overalls.

"Thought you'd be coming in this morning," he told Eliot

"I told you I was going over to Falmouth."

"Any luck?"

"A 933 Bentley."

"What sort of condition?"

"Looked OK. A bit of rust."

"Get the old paint spray out. There was a chap in the other day, wanting one of them."

"I know, that's why I bought it. Thought we'd take the transporter over, tomorrow or the next day, pick her up."

They fell silent. Morris went to his transistor

and turned it on again, if anything louder than before. I looked down at the confusion of engineering on which he had been working and finally asked Eliot what sort of a car it had originally been.

"A 1971 Jaguar XJ6 4.2 litre, if you really want to know. And it will be again when Morris has finished with it. This is another that was in a crash."

Morris came back to stand between us.

"What exactly are you doing to it?" I asked him.

"Straightening out the chassis, fixing the wheel alignment."

"What about the brake shoes?" said Eliot.

"It could have done with new brake shoes, but I fixed the old ones to cover us for the guarantee . . . and Mr Kemback rang up from Birmingham . . ."

They began to talk shop. I drifted away, deafened by the sound of rock, went back through the showroom and out into the forecourt where Rufus waited, with dignity and patience, behind the driving wheel of Eliot's car. Together we sat there until we were rejoined by Eliot. "Sorry about that, Rebecca; I wanted to check on another job. Morris is a good mechanic, but he gets shirty if he's expected to answer the telephone as well."

"Who's Mr Kemback? Another customer?"

"No, not exactly. He was down here last summer on holiday. He runs a motel, a garage, just off the M6. He's got quite a selection of old cars. Wants to start a museum, you know, a sort of sideline to the bacon-and-egg trade. He seems to want me to run it for him."

"You mean go and live in Birmingham?"

"Doesn't sound very tempting, does it? Anyway, that's it. Let's go and look at my mother's house."

We walked there, just a little way down the street, then up a short lane and through a double white gate, and the path sloped up to a long, low white house, which had been converted from two ancient thick-walled stone cottages. Eliot took a key out of his pocket and opened the door and inside it was cold, but not musty or damp. It was furnished like an expensive London flat, with pale, thick, fitted carpets and pale walls and sofas upholstered in mushroom-coloured brocade. There were a great many mirrors and little crystal bag chandeliers hanging from the low-beamed ceilings.

It was all charming, and just what I had imagined, and somehow wrong. A kitchen like an advertisement, a dining room furnished with gleaming mahogany, upstairs there were four bedrooms and three bathrooms, a sewing room and a linen cupboard of mammoth proportions, richly smelling of soap.

At the back of the house was a little patio, and then a long garden sloped up to a distant hedge. I looked at the patio and could see Mollie out there, entertaining her friends, with cane furniture set out on the flagstones, and martinis to drink, served from an expensive glass trolley.

I said, "It's a perfect house," and meant it. But I did not love it as I loved Boscarva. Perhaps because it was too perfect.

We stood in the elegant out-of-place drawing

room and eyed each other. Our day together seemed to have come to an end. Perhaps Eliot felt this too and wanted to postpone it, for he said, "I could put on a kettle and make you a cup of tea, only I know that there's no milk in the fridge."

"I think we should go home." I was surprised by an enormous yawn, and Eliot laughed at me. He took my shoulders between his hands. "You're sleepy."

"Too much fresh air," I answered. "Too much wine."

I tipped my head back to look up into his face, and we were very close. I could feel his fingers tighten over my shoulders. He wasn't laughing any more, but his deep-set eyes held an expression as gentle as anything I had ever seen.

I said, "It's been a wonderful day . . ." but that was as far as I got, because he kissed me then, and for some time I was not able to say anything at all. When at last he drew away I was so shaken that all I could do was lean limply against him, wanting to cry, feeling a fool, knowing that the situation was fast slipping out of my control. My cheek was against his coat, and his arms around me held me so close that I could feel, like the throb of a drum, the solid beating of his heart.

Over the top of my head, I heard him say, "You mustn't go back to London. You mustn't ever go away again."

9

The shopping which I had done in Falmouth
proved to be an unexpected blessing. I must have
been inspired, for, without thinking, I provided exactly the small talking point we all needed to smooth
over the embarrassment of the previous uncomfortable evening. Mollie was charmed with her freesias;
she couldn't grow them at Boscarva, she explained,
the winds were too cold, the garden too exposed. She
paid me the compliment of arranging them with
more artistry than one would have thought possible,
and finally giving them the place of honour in the
middle of the mantelpiece in the drawing room. They
filled the room with their rich romantic scent, and
the cream and the violet and the deep pink drew
one's eye, quite naturally, up to the portrait of Sophia. The flowers seemed to complement the glowing
skin tones and the fragile shimmer of the white dress.

"Beautiful," said Mollie, standing back, but I
could not be sure whether she was referring to the
flowers or the portrait. "It was sweet of you to bring
them. And did Eliot take you to see my house? So

now you can understand how I feel about having to live in this great place." She regarded me thoughtfully, her eyes narrowed. "You know, I believe the day has done you good. I could even imagine you've caught the sun. You've got quite a good colour. The air must agree with you."

Pettifer accepted his sherry with dignity, but I could tell that he was pleased. And Grenville was wickedly delighted with his cigars, for the doctor had warned him against smoking and Pettifer had hidden his usual supply. I understood that he was parsimonious about doling them out. Grenville took and lit one instantly, puffing away with immense satisfaction and leaning back in his big chair like a man without a care in the world. Even with Andrea I had for once done the right thing. *The Creepers!* How did you know they're my favourite group? Oh, I wish there was a record player here, but there isn't and I left mine in London. Gosh, aren't they fabulous, groovy . . . ?" And then she came down to earth again, searching for the price tag. "That must have cost you something."

It was as though, with peace offerings, we had all formed an unspoken pact. Last night was never discussed. There was no mention of the davenport desk, of Ernest Padlow, of the possible sale of Boscarva Farm. There was no mention of Joss. After dinner Eliot set up a table, and Mollie got out the rosewood box containing the mah-jongg set, and we played until bed time, Andrea sitting with Mollie in order to learn the rules.

I caught myself thinking that, if a stranger were
to come, unexpectedly, upon us, how he would be
charmed by the picture we made, caught, like flies in
amber, in the pool of light from the standard lamp,
absorbed by our timeless occupation. The distin-
guished painter, mellow in the twilight of his years,
surrounded by his family; the pretty daughter-in-law
and the handsome grandson—and even Andrea, for
once alert and interested, absorbed by the intricacies
of the game.

I had played as a child with my mother, sometimes making up a foursome with two of her friends,
and found myself comforted by the remembered
touch of the ivory and bamboo tiles, by their beauty,
and the satisfying sound they made, like sea pebbles
disturbed by the tide, as we stirred them around in
the middle of the table.

At the start of each round we built the four
walls, two tiles high, and closed them together into a
tight square, "to keep the evil spirits out," we were
told by Grenville, who had learned to play as a young
Sub-Lieutenant in Hong Kong and knew all the
traditional superstitions of the ancient game. I
thought how easy it would be, how safe, if ghosts and
doubts and skeletons-in-the-cupboard could be thus
shut out and kept at bay.

The travel brochures and holiday posters of
Porthkerris inevitably portrayed a place where the
sea and the sky were always a bright and unsullied
blue, the houses white with sunshine, the odd palm

tree in the foreground lending that suggestion of Mediterranean glamour. The imagination was led, naturally, to visions of fresh lobster, eaten out of doors; artists with beards and paint-stained smocks; and weather-beaten fishermen, picturesque as pirates, sitting on bollards, smoking their pipes and discussing last week's catch.

But Porthkerris, in February, in a north-east gale, had no shred of connection with this nebulous paradise.

The sea, the sky, the very town were grey, the maze of baffling, narrow streets subjected to onslaughts of bitter wind. The tide was high; the waves broke against the sea-wall and splashed across the road, misting the windows of the houses opposite with salt, and filling the gutters with yellow foam, like dirty soapsuds.

It was as though the place were under some sort of a siege. Shoppers were wrapped, buttoned, scarved in every sort of protective clothing, their faces half hidden by hoods or deep coat collars, their bodies bundled into ambiguity, so that men and women all looked alike, gumbooted and shapeless.

The sky was the colour of the wind, the air filled with flying flotsam, old leaves, twigs, scraps of paper, even tiles torn from roofs. In the shops, people forgot what they had come to buy, the talk was all of the weather, the wind, the damage the storm was going to do.

I had come, once more, to shop for Mollie, fighting my way down the hill in borrowed raincoat and rubber boots, because I felt safer on my feet than I would have driving Mollie's insubstantial car. Now that I was more familiar with the town I no longer needed Andrea to show me the way . . . anyway Andrea was still in bed when I left Boscarva, and for once I did not blame her. The day was not inviting and it was hard to believe that only yesterday I had been sitting out, in my shirtsleeves, basking in a sun as warm as May.

The last of the shopping completed, I emerged from the baker's as the clock in the tower of the Norman church struck eleven. Normally, under such conditions, I would have headed straight back up the hill to Boscarva, but I had other plans. With my head down, the heavy basket over one arm, I made for the harbour.

The Art Gallery, I knew, was housed in an old Baptist Chapel, somewhere in the maze of streets which lay to the north of the town. I had thought that I would simply go and look for it, but as I braved the harbour road, battling with alternate assaults of wind and spray, I saw the old fisherman's lodge which had been converted to a Tourist Information Bureau and decided that I would save myself both time and effort if I made a few inquiries.

Inside, I found an unenthusiastic girl huddled over a paraffin stove; booted and shivering, she looked like the sole survivor of some Arctic expedition. When I appeared she did not move from her chair but said, "Yes?" and stared at me through a pair of unbecoming spectacles.

I tried to feel sorry for her. "I'm looking for the Art Gallery."

"Which one did you want?"

"I didn't know there was more than one."

Behind me the door opened and shut and we were joined by a third person. The girl looked over my shoulder and a faint interest gleamed behind her pebble glasses.

"There's the Town Gallery and the New Painters," she said, much more lively.

"I don't know which I want."

"Perhaps," said a voice behind me, "I can help."

I swung around and Joss stood there, in rubber boots and a streaming black oilskin, a fisherman's cap jammed down on to his head. His face was wet with rain, his hands jammed into the deep pockets of the coat, his dark eyes glinting with amusement. One half of me could see exactly why the sluggish girl behind the counter had suddenly come to life. The other half was maddened by his extraordinary ability to turn up just when I was least expecting him.

I remembered Andrea. I remembered the desk and the chair. I said, coolly, "Hallo, Joss."

"I saw you come in. What are you wanting to do?"

The girl chipped in. "She wants the Art Gallery."

Joss waited for me to enlarge on this and, thus cornered, I did so.

"I thought perhaps there might be some pictures of Grenville's there . . ."

"You're quite right, there are three. I'll take you . . ."

"I don't need to be taken, I just want to be told how to get there."

"I'd like to take you . . . here—" he removed my heavy basket from my arm, smiled at the girl and went to open the door. A howl of wind and a blast of spume-laden air poured in from the outside and a pile of leaflets flew and scattered from the counter all over the floor. Before we could do any more damage, I hurried out, and the door swung shut behind us. As though it were the most natural thing in the world, Joss took my arm and we made our way down the middle of the cobbled road, Joss carrying on a cheerful conversation despite the fact that the wind tore the words from his mouth, and that, even with his arm in mine, it was taking all my efforts to progress at all.

"What on earth brings you down to the town on a day like this?"

"You're carrying it. Mollie's shopping."

"Couldn't you have brought the car?"

"I thought I might get blown off the road."

"I love it," he told me. "I love a day like this." He looked as though he loved it too, wind-whipped and wet and bursting with vitality. "Did you have a good day yesterday?"

"What do you know about yesterday?"

"I was up at Boscarva and Andrea told me you'd gone to Falmouth with Eliot. Don't imagine you can keep any secrets in this place. If Andrea hadn't told me, Pettifer would, or Mrs Thomas, or Mrs Kernow, or Miss Bright-Eyes in the Information Bureau. It's part of the fun of living in Porthkerris, everybody knows exactly what everybody else is up to."

"I'm beginning to realize that."

We turned away from the harbour and began to climb a steep cobbled hill. Houses closed in on either side of us, a cat flashed across the street and disappeared through a crack in a window. A woman in a pot hat and a blue apron was scrubbing her steps. She looked up and saw us, and said, " 'Ullo my lover," to Joss; her fingers were like a bunch of pink sausages, made so by the hot water and the cold wind.

At the end of the street, we found ourselves in a little square which I had not seen before. One side of this was taken up by a large barn-like structure, with arched windows set high along the wall. By the door was a sign, PORTHKERRIS ART GALLERY, and Joss let go of my arm, pushed open the door with his shoulder and stood aside to let me go ahead of him. Inside it was bitterly cold, draughty, totally empty. The white walls were hung with paintings, of all sorts and shapes and sizes, and two great abstract sculptures were marooned in the middle of the floor, like rocks exposed by an ebb tide. There was a table by the door, with neat stacks of catalogues and folders and copies of *The Studio,* but despite this window-dressing the gallery stayed thick with the atmosphere of joyless bygone Sundays.

"Now," Joss put down my basket and took off

his cap, shaking it free of rain as a dog shakes its coat, "what do you want to see?"

"I want to see Sophia."

He glanced at me sharply with a sudden turn of his head, but in the same instant smiled and put his hat on his head again, pulling the peak down over his eyes, like a guardsman.

"Who told you about Sophia?"

I smiled sweetly. "Perhaps it was Mrs Thomas. Perhaps it was Mrs Kernow. Perhaps it was Miss Bright-Eyes in the Information Bureau."

"Insolence will get you nowhere."

"There *is* a portrait of Sophia here. Pettifer told me."

"Yes. It's over this way."

I followed him down the length of the floor, our rubber-booted footsteps sounding loud in the emptiness.

"There," he said. I stopped beside him and looked up, and she was there, sitting in a beam of lamplight with some sewing in her hands.

I stared at it for a long time and finally let out a long sigh of disappointment. Joss looked down at me from under the ridiculous peak of his cap.

"What's that sigh for?"

"You still can't see her face. I still don't know what she looks like. Why didn't he ever paint her face?"

"He did. Often."

"Well, I still haven't seen it. It's always the back of her head, or her hands, or else she's so small a part of the picture she doesn't have a face at all, just a blob."

"Does it matter what she looked like?"

"No, it doesn't matter. It's just that I want to know."

"How did you know about Sophia in the first place?"

"My mother told me about her. And then Pettifer, and the picture of her—the one at Boscarva in the drawing room—is so charming and feminine, one feels she must have been beautiful. But Pettifer says that she wasn't beautiful at all. Just very charming and attractive." We looked again at the picture. I saw the hands, and the shine of lamplight on her dark hair. "Pettifer says that art galleries up and down the country have portraits of Sophia hanging on their walls. I shall just have to go on from Manchester to Birmingham, to Nottingham, to Glasgow, until I find one that isn't of the back of her head."

"What will you do then?"

"Nothing. Just know what she looks like."

I turned from my disappointment and began to walk back to the door where my laden basket waited for me, but Joss was there first, stooping to swing it up and out of my reach.

I said, "I must go back."

"It's only—" he consulted his watch—"half past eleven. And you've never seen my shop. Come back with me and let me show it off, and I'll make you a cup of coffee and drive you home. You can't possibly walk up the hill with this great weight on your arm."

"Of course I can."

"I won't let you." He opened the door. "Come along."

I couldn't go without the basket and he obviously wasn't going to give it up, so, resigned and reluctant, I went with him, pushing my hands into my pockets so that he could not take my arm. He seemed in no way put out by my ungraciousness, which in itself was disconcerting, but when we got back to the harbour and were once more in the teeth of the wind, I nearly lost my balance with the unexpectedness of it, and he laughed and pulled my hand out of my pocket, taking it in his own. It was hard not to be disarmed by this protective and forgiving gesture.

As soon as the shop came in view, the tall narrow house shouldering up between the two short fat ones, I saw that indeed changes had taken place. The window frames were now painted, the plate glass had been cleaned, and a sign put up over the door. JOSS GARDNER.

"How does that look?" He was full of pride.

"Impressive," I had to admit.

He took a key out of his pocket and unlocked the door and we went into the shop. Packing cases stood about on the flagged floor, and around the walls, shelving was being erected in varying widths, up to the ceiling. In the centre of the room was another structure, rather like a child's climbing frame, and this had already been set out with modern Danish glass and china, cooking pots in bright colours,

and brightly striped Indian rugs. The walls were
white, the woodwork had been left in its natural
state, and this and the grey floor provided a simple
and effective background to the bright wares which
he had to sell. At the back of the shop an open staircase rose to the upper floors, and beneath this was
another door, ajar, leading down into what appeared
to be a dark cellar. "Come upstairs . . ." He led the
way.

I followed him. "What's that door there?"

"That's my workshop. It's in a dreadful mess,
I'll show you that another time. Now this—" we
emerged on to the first floor, and could scarcely move
for baskets and wickerwork—"I haven't exactly got
this straight but, as you can see, this is where you buy
baskets for logs, clothes pegs, shopping, babies, laun-
dry, anything you care to put in them."

None of it was very spacious. The narrow house
was just a glorified staircase with a landing on each
floor.

"Up again. How are your legs? Now we come to
the *pièce de résistance,* the owner's palatial living
quarters." I passed a tiny bathroom squeezed into the
turn of the stairs. And lagging behind Joss's long legs
found myself remembering Andrea's yearning de-
scriptions of his flat, and hoping it would not be the
way she had described it to me, but entirely different,
so that I would know that her imagination had taken
control, and that she had made the whole thing up.

Just like something out of a magazine. With a

bed that's a sort of sofa and masses of cushions and things and a log fire.

But it was just the way she had said. As I came up the last stairs, my fleeting hope swiftly died. And there *was* something closed-in and secret about it, with the ceiling sloping down to the floor and a dormer window set into the gable with a seat below it. I saw the little galley, enclosed behind a counter, like a bar, and the old Turkish carpet on the floor, and the divan, red-blanketed, pushed against the wall. As she had said, it was scattered with cushions.

Joss had put down my basket and was already divesting himself of his wet clothes and hanging them on an old-fashioned cane hat-stand.

"Take your things off before you die of cold," he told me. "I'll light a fire . . ."

"I can't stay, Joss . . ."

"No reason not to light the fire. And please, take off that coat."

I did, unbuttoning it with frozen fingers, pulling off my damp woollen hat and shaking my plait down over my shoulder. While I hung these up beside Joss's things, he was busy at the fireplace, snapping twigs, balling paper, scraping together the ashes from some previous fire, lighting it all with a long taper. When it was crackling he took some pieces of driftwood, tar-soaked, from a basket by the fireplace, and stacked them round the flames. They spat, and spluttered, and swiftly caught. And the room, by firelight, sprang to life. He stood up and turned to face me.

"Now, what do you want? Coffee? Tea? Chocolate? Brandy and soda?"

"Coffee?"

"Two coffees coming up." He retired behind his counter, filled a kettle and lit the gas. As he collected a tray and cups, I went over to the window, knelt on the seat and looked down through the fury of the storm to the street below, washed by spray as the waves broke over the sea wall. The boats in the harbour bobbed about like demented corks, and huge herring gulls floated over their swinging mastheads, screaming at the wind. Absorbed in the task of making our coffee, Joss moved with economy from one side of the galley to the other, neat-fingered and self-sufficient as a single-minded yachtsman. So occupied, he appeared harmless enough, but the disconcerting point about Andrea's revelations was that they all seemed to contain an element of truth.

I had known Joss for only a few days, but already I had seen him in every sort of mood. I knew he could be charming, stubborn, angry, and downright rude. It was not difficult to imagine him as a ruthless and passionate lover, but it was distasteful to imagine him with Andrea.

He looked up suddenly and caught my eye. I was embarrassed, caught with my thoughts. I said, quickly, to divert us both, "In good weather you must have a lovely view."

"Clear out to the lighthouse."

"In the summer it must be like being abroad."

"In the summer it's like Piccadilly Underground

at rush hour. But that only lasts for two months." He came out from behind his counter, carrying a tray with the steaming cups, the sugar bowl and the milk jug. The coffee smelt delicious. He pulled forward a long stool with his foot, set the tray at one end of it and himself at the other. Thus, we faced each other.

"I want to hear more about yesterday," said Joss. "Where did you go besides Falmouth?"

I told him about St Endon and the little pub by the water's edge.

"Yes, I've heard about it, but I've never been there. Did you get a good lunch?"

"Yes. And it was so warm that we sat out in the sunshine."

"That's the south coast for you. And what happened then?"

"Nothing happened then. We came home."

He handed me my cup and saucer. "Did Eliot take you to High Cross?"

"Yes."

"Did you see the garage?"

"Yes. And Mollie's house."

"What did you think of all those elegant, sexy cars?"

"I thought just that. That they were elegant and sexy."

"Did you meet any of the guys who work for him?"

His voice was so casual that I became wary.

"Who, for instance?"

"Morris Tatcombe?"

"Joss, you didn't ask me here for coffee at all, did you? You're pumping me."

"I'm not. I promise I'm not. It's just that I wondered if Morris was working for Eliot."

"What do you know about Morris?"

"Just that he's rotten."

"He's a good mechanic."

"Yes, he is. Everybody knows that, and it's the only good thing about him. But he's also totally dishonest and vicious to boot."

"If he's totally dishonest, why isn't he in jail?"

"He's already been. He's just come out."

This took the wind out of my sails, but I soldiered bravely on, sounding more sure of myself than I felt.

"And how do you know he's vicious . . . ?"

"Because he picked a quarrel with me one night in a pub. We went outside and I punched him in the nose, and it was lucky for me I hit him first, because he was carrying a knife."

"Why are you telling me this?"

"Because you asked. If you don't want to be told things, you shouldn't ask questions."

"And what am I meant to do about it?"

"Nothing. Absolutely nothing. I'm sorry I brought it up. It was just that I'd heard Eliot had given him a job and I hoped it wasn't true."

"You don't like Eliot, do you?"

"I don't like him, I don't dislike him. He's nothing to do with me. But I'll tell you something. He picks bad friends."

"You mean Ernest Padlow?"

Joss sent me a glance that was full of reluctant admiration.

"You don't waste much time, I'll say that for you. You seem to know it all."

"I know about Ernest Padlow because I saw him with Eliot that first night when you gave me dinner at The Anchor."

"So you did. That's another rotten egg. If Ernest had his way the whole of Porthkerris would be bulldozed into car parks. There wouldn't be a house left standing. And we would all have to go up the hill and live in his fancy little semis which in ten years' time will be leaking, leaning, cracking up and generally bagging at the knees."

I did not reply to this outburst. I drank my coffee and thought how pleasant it would be to have a conversation without being instantly drawn into longstanding vendettas which had nothing to do with me. I was tired of listening to everybody I wanted to like running down the reputations of everybody else.

I finished my coffee, set down the cup and said, "I must get back."

Joss, with an obvious effort, apologized. "I'm sorry."

"Why?"

"For losing my temper."

"Eliot's my cousin, Joss."

"I know." He looked down, turning his cup in his hands. "But, without meaning to, I've become involved with Boscarva, too."

"Just don't take your prejudices out on me."

His eyes met mine. "I wasn't angry with you."

"I know." I stood up. "I must go," I said again.

"I'll drive you back."

"You don't have to . . ." But he paid no attention to my protest, just took my coat from its hook and helped me on with it. I pulled the wet woollen hat over my ears and picked up the heavy basket.

The telephone rang.

Joss, in his oilskin, went to answer it, and I started downstairs. I heard him call, just before he took the receiver off the hook, "Rebecca, wait for me. I won't be a moment . . ." and then, into the telephone, "Yes? Yes, Joss Gardner here . . ."

I went down to the ground floor and the shop. It was still raining. Upstairs I could hear Joss deep in conversation.

Bored with waiting for him, perhaps a little curious, I pushed open the door of the workshop, turned on the light, and went down four stone steps. There was the usual confusion, benches, woodshavings, scraps, tools, vises; over all hung the smell of glue, of new wood, of polish. There was also a clutter of old furniture, so dusty and ramshackle it was impossible to tell whether it was of any value or not. A chest of drawers missing all its handles, a bedside cupboard without a leg.

And then, at the very back of the room, in the shadows, I saw them. A davenport desk, in apparently perfect repair, and alongside it a chair in the

Chinese Chippendale style, with a tapestry seat, embroidered in flowers.

I felt sick, as though I had been kicked in the stomach. I turned and went up the steps, turning off the light and closing the door, going through the shop and out into the bitter windblast of that wicked February day.

My workshop's in a dreadful mess, I'll show you that another time.

I walked and then found that I was running up towards the church, into a warren of little lanes where he would never find me. I was running, always uphill, encumbered by the shopping basket, heavy as lead, and my heart pounded in my chest and there was the taste of blood in my mouth.

Eliot had been right. It was too easy for Joss and he had simply taken his chance. It was my desk; it was *my* desk that he had taken, but he had taken it from Grenville's house, flinging the old man's trust and kindness back in his face.

I could imagine killing Joss, and it was easy. I told myself that I could never speak to him, could never bear to be near him again. I had never been so angry in my life. With him; but worse with myself, for having been taken in by his empty charm, for having been proved so totally wrong. I had never been so angry.

I stumbled on up the hill.

But if I was so angry, then why was I crying?

10

It was a long and exhausting climb back to Boscarva, and I have never found it possible to sustain extreme emotion for more than ten minutes. Gradually, fighting my way up the hill against the weather, I calmed down, wiped my tears away with my gloved hand, pulled myself together. In an apparently intolerable situation, there is nearly always something one can do, and long before I reached Boscarva I had decided what it was. I would go back to London.

I left the shopping basket on the kitchen table and went upstairs to my room, took off all my drenched clothes, changed my shoes, washed my hands, carefully re-plaited my hair; thus calmed I went in search of Grenville and found him in his study, sitting by the fire and reading the morning paper.

He lowered this and looked over the top of it as I came in.

"Rebecca."

"Hallo. How are you this wild morning?" I

sounded determinedly cheerful, like a maddening nurse.

"Full of aches and pains. The wind's a killer even if you never go out in it. Where've you been?"

"Down in Porthkerris. I had to do some shopping for Mollie."

"What time is it?"

"Half past twelve."

"Then let's have a glass of sherry."

"Is that allowed?"

"I don't give a damn if it's allowed or not. You know where the decanter is."

I poured two glasses, carried his over and set it carefully down on the table by his chair. I pulled up a stool and sat facing him. I said, "Grenville, I have to go back to London."

"What?"

"I have to go back to London." The blue eyes narrowed, the great jaw thrust out; I hastily made Stephen Forbes my scapegoat. "I can't stay away for ever. I've already been away from work nearly two weeks, and Stephen Forbes, the man I work for, he's been so good about it, I can't just go on taking advantage of his kindness and generosity. I've just realized that it's Friday already. I must go back to London this weekend. I must be back at work on Monday morning."

"But you've only just come." He was obviously thoroughly disgusted with me.

"I've been here three days. After three days fish and guests stink."

"You're not a guest. You're Lisa's child."

"But I still have commitments. And I like my job and I don't want to stop working." I smiled, trying to divert him. "And now I've found the way to Boscarva, perhaps I can come again, when I've got more time to spare, to spend with you."

He did not reply but sat, looking old and grumpy, staring into the fire.

He said dismally, "I may not be here then."

"Oh, of course you will be."

He sighed, took a slow, shaky mouthful of sherry, set down his glass, and turned to me, apparently resigned.

"When do you want to go?"

I was surprised, but relieved, that he had given in so easily.

"Perhaps tomorrow night. I'll get a sleeper. And then I can have Sunday to get myself settled into my flat."

"You shouldn't be living in a flat in London on your own. You weren't made for living alone. You were made for a man, and a home, and children. If I were twenty years younger and could still paint, that's how I'd show you to the world, in a field or a garden, knee-deep in buttercups and children."

"Perhaps it'll happen one day. And then I shall send for you."

His face was suddenly full of pain. He turned away from me and said, "I wish you'd stay."

I longed to say that I would, but there were a

thousand reasons why I couldn't. "I'll come back," I promised.

He made a great and touching effort to pull himself together, clearing his throat, re-settling himself in his chair. "That jade of yours. We'll have to get Pettifer to pack it in a box, then you can take it with you. And the mirror . . . could you manage that on the train, or is it too big? You ought to have a car, then there would be no problems. Have you got a car?"

"No, but it doesn't matter . . ."

"And I suppose that desk hasn't . . ."

"It doesn't matter about the desk!" I interrupted, so loudly and so suddenly that Grenville looked at me in some surprise, as though he had not expected such bad manners.

"I'm sorry," I said quickly. "It's just that it really doesn't matter. I couldn't bear everybody to start quarrelling about it again. Please, for my sake, don't talk about it, don't think about it any more."

He regarded me thoughtfully, a long unblinking stare that made me drop my eyes.

He said, "You think I'm unfair to Eliot?"

"I just think that perhaps you never talk to each other, you never tell each other anything."

"He'd have been different if Roger hadn't been killed. He was a boy who needed a father."

"Couldn't you have done as a father?"

"Could never get near him for Mollie. He was never made to stick to anything. Always chopping and changing jobs and then he started that garage up three years ago."

"That seems to be a success."

"Second-hand cars!" His voice was full of unjustified contempt. "He should have gone into the Navy."

"Suppose he didn't want to go into the Navy?"

"He might have, if his mother hadn't talked him out of it. She wanted to keep him at home, tied to her apron strings."

"Oh, Grenville, I think you're being thoroughly old-fashioned and very unfair."

"Did I ask you for your opinion?" But already he was cheering up. A good argument was, to Grenville, like a shot in the arm.

"I don't care whether you asked for it or not, you've got it."

He laughed then, and reached forward to gently pinch my cheek. He said, "How I wish I could still paint. Do you still want one of my pictures to take back to London with you?"

I was afraid that he had forgotten. "More than anything."

"You can get the key of the studio from Pettifer. Tell him I said you could have it. Go and nose around, see what you can find."

"You won't come with me?"

Again the pain came into his face. "No," he said gruffly, and turned away to take up his sherry. He sat, looking down at the amber wine, turning the glass in his hand. "No, I won't come with you."

* * *

At lunch he broke the news to the others. Andrea, livid that I was going back to London while she had to stay in horrible, boring Cornwall, went into a sullen sulk. But the others were gratifyingly dismayed.

"But do you have to go?" That was Mollie.

"Yes, I really must. I've got a job to do and I can't stay away for ever."

"We really love having you here." She could be charming when she wasn't aggressive and possessive about Eliot, resentful of Grenville and Boscarva. I saw her again as a pretty little cat, but now I was aware of long claws hidden in the soft velvet paws, and I knew that she had no compunction about using them.

"I've loved it too . . ."

Pettifer was more outspoken. After lunch I went out to the kitchen to help him with the dishes, and he minced no words.

"What you want to go away for now, just when you're settling down and the Commander's getting to know you—well, it's beyond me. I didn't think you were that sort of a person . . ."

"I'll come back. I've said I'll come back."

"He's eighty now. He's not going to last for ever. How are you going to feel, coming back and him not here, but six feet under the ground and pushing up the daisies?"

"Oh, Pettifer, *don't.*"

"It's all very well saying 'Oh, Pettifer, *don't.*' There's nothing I can do about it."

"I've got a job. I must go back."

"Sounds like selfishness to me."

"That's not fair."

"All these years he's not seen his daughter, and then you turn up and stay three days. What sort of a grandchild are you?"

I didn't reply because there was nothing to say. And I hated feeling guilty and being put in the wrong. We finished the dishes in silence, but when they were done and he was wiping down the draining board with a damp cloth, I tried to make my peace with him.

"I'm sorry. I really am. It's bad enough having to go without you making me feel a brute. And I will come back. I've said I will. Perhaps in the summer . . . he'll still be here in the summer, and the weather will be warm and we can do things together. Perhaps you could take us out in the car . . ."

My voice trailed away. Pettifer hung his cloth neatly over the edge of the sink. He said, gruffly, "The Commander said you were to have the key of the studio. Don't know what you'll find down there. A lot of dust and spiders, I should think."

"He said I could have a picture. He said I could go and choose one."

He slowly dried his worn, gnarled hands. "I'll have to find the key. It's put away for safe keeping. Didn't want it lying around where anyone could get their hands on it. There's a lot of good stuff down in the studio."

"Any time will do." I could not bear his disapproval. "Oh, Pettifer, don't be angry with me."

He melted then. "Oh, I'm not angry. Perhaps it's me who's being selfish. Perhaps it's me who doesn't want you to go."

I saw him suddenly, not as the ubiquitous Pettifer around whom this household revolved, but as an old man, nearly as old as my grandfather and probably as lonely. A stupid lump came into my throat and for a terrible moment I thought I was going to burst into tears, which would have made it the second time that day, but then Pettifer said, "And don't go choosing one of them nudes, they wouldn't be suitable," and the dangerous moment was behind me and we were smiling, friends again.

That afternoon Mollie lent me her car, and I drove the five miles to the railway junction and there bought myself a ticket back to London and reserved a sleeper for the night train on Saturday. The violence of the wind had dropped a little, but it was still wild and stormy, with trees down and devastation everywhere, smashed greenhouses, broken branches, and fields of early spring bulbs flattened by the gales.

I got home to find Mollie in the garden at Boscarva, bundled up against the weather (even Mollie could not look elegant on such a day) and trying to tie up and rescue some of the more fragile shrubs that grew around the house. When she saw the car, she decided to call it a day, for as I put it away and walked back towards the house I met her coming towards me, stripping off her gloves and tucking a strand of hair into her head-scarf.

"I can't bear it a moment longer," she told me. "I hate wind, it exhausts me. But that darling little daphne was being snapped to ribbons, and all the camellias have been burnt by this wind. It turns them quite brown. Let's go in and have a cup of tea."

While she changed I put the kettle on, and set out cups on a tray. "Where is everybody?" I asked her when she reappeared, miraculously neat once more, down to her pearls and her matching ear-rings.

"Grenville's having a nap and Andrea's up in her room . . ." she sighed. ". . . I must say, she really isn't the easiest of girls. If only she'd do something to amuse herself instead of skulking around in this tiresome manner. I'm afraid it's not doing her any good being down here, I didn't think it would, to be quite honest, but my poor sister was quite desperate." She looked around the comfortable kitchen. "This is cosy. Let's have our tea in here. The drawing room's so draughty when the wind's from the sea, and we can scarcely draw the curtains at half past four in the afternoon . . ."

She was right, it was cosy in the kitchen. She found a cloth and laid the tea, setting out cakes and biscuits, sugar bowl and silver milk jug. Even for kitchen tea, it appeared, her standards were meticulous. She pulled up two wheel-back chairs, and was in the act of reaching for the teapot when the door opened and Andrea appeared.

"Oh, Andrea, dear, just in time. We're having kitchen tea today. Do you want a cup?"

"I'm sorry, I haven't got time."

This unexpectedly mannerly reply made Mollie look up sharply. "Are you going out?"

"Yes," said Andrea, "I'm going to the cinema."

We both stared at her like fools. For the impossible had happened—Andrea had suddenly decided to take much trouble with her appearance. She had washed her hair and tied it back off her face, found a clean polo-necked tee-shirt, and even, I was delighted to see, a bra to wear beneath it. Her Celtic cross hung around her neck on its thread of leather, her black jeans were neatly pressed, her clumpy shoes polished. Over her arm was a raincoat and a fringed leather handbag. I had never seen her look so presentable. And, best of all, the expression on her face was neither sulky nor malevolent, but . . . demure? Could one possibly describe Andrea as looking demure?

"I mean," she went on, "if that's all right by you, Auntie Mollie."

"Well, of course. What are you going to see?"

"*Mary of Scotland.* It's on at the Plaza."

"Are you going by yourself?"

"No, I'm going with Joss. He rang me while you were out gardening. He's going to give me supper afterwards."

"Oh," said Mollie, faintly. And then, feeling that further comment was expected of her, ". . . how are you going to get down there?"

"I'll walk down, and I expect Joss will drive me home . . ."

"Have you got some money?"

"I've got 50p. I'll be all right."

"Well . . ." But Mollie was defeated. "Have a good time."

"I will," she flashed us both a smile. "Goodbye."

The door swung to behind her.

"Goodbye," said Mollie. She looked at me. "Extraordinary," she said.

I was concentrating on my cup of tea. "Why so extraordinary?" I said casually.

"Andrea and . . . Joss. I mean he's always been quite polite to her, but . . . to ask her out . . . ?"

"You shouldn't sound so surprised. She's attractive when she cleans herself up and bothers to smile. Probably she smiles at Joss all the time."

"You think it's all right, letting her go? I mean I do have responsibilities . . . ?"

"Honestly, I don't see how you could have stopped her going. Anyway she's seventeen, she's not a child. She can surely look after herself by now . . ."

"That's just the trouble," said Mollie . . . "That's always been the trouble with Andrea."

"She'll be all right."

She would not be all right, and I knew this, but I could not disillusion Mollie. Besides, what did it matter? It was no business of mine if Joss chose to spend his evenings making firelit love to an adolescent nymphomaniac. They were two of a kind. They deserved each other. They were welcome to each other.

When we had finished tea, Mollie tied a neat apron around her waist and started preparing dinner. I cleared away the cups and saucers and washed them up. As I was drying the last plate, and putting it away, Pettifer appeared, bearing in his hand a large key which looked as though it might unlock a dungeon.

"I knew I'd put it somewhere safely, found it in the back of a drawer in the Commander's bureau . . ."

"What's that, Pettifer?" Mollie asked.

"The key to the studio, Madam . . ."

"Heavens, who wants that?"

"I do," I said. "Grenville said I could go down and choose a picture to take back to London."

"My dear child, what a task you'll have. The place must be in the most terrible mess, it hasn't seen the light of day for ten years."

"I don't mind." I took the key which weighed heavy as lead in my hand.

"Are you going now? It's getting dark."

"Aren't there any lights?"

"Oh, yes, of course, but it's very cheerless. Wait till tomorrow morning."

But I wanted to go now. "I'll be all right. I'll put on a coat."

"There's a torch on the hall table, you'd better take that as well, the path down the garden is quite steep and slippery."

And so, buttoned into my leather coat, and armed with the torch and the key, I set off, letting myself out of the house by the garden door. The wind from the sea was still violent, carrying with it squalls of thin, cold rain, and I had to struggle to get the door closed behind me. The dismal afternoon was turning early to darkness, but still there was enough light to pick my way cautiously down the sloping garden, and I did not turn on the torch until I reached the studio when I needed its beam to find the keyhole.

I fitted the key and it turned reluctantly, needing oil; the door swung inwards, creakingly. There was a damp and musty smell, a suggestion of cobwebs and mould, and I quickly put my hand inside and felt for the light switch. At once a single naked bulb, high in the roof, sprang to a chill and insubstantial life, and I was surrounded by leaping shadows, for the draught caused the long flex to swing to and fro like the pendulum of a clock.

I went in and shut the door behind me and the shadows, slowly, were stilled. Around me, dust-covered shapes loomed in the half-light, but across the room was a standard lamp, with a crooked, broken shade. I picked my way over to this, found the switch and turned that on, and at once everything looked a little less forlorn.

I saw that the studio had been designed on two levels with a sleeping gallery at the south end, reached by a stair like a ship's ladder.

I went half-way up the ladder and saw the divan

and the striped blanket. Over the bed was a window
tightly shuttered, and a pillow had shed feathers, perhaps the work of some marauding mouse. The re-
mains of a small dead bird lay, twig-like and dehy-
drated, in the corner of the floor. I shuddered slightly
at the desolation, and descended again to the studio.

The wind banged and rattled at the huge north
window. A complicated contraption of strings and
pulleys worked the long curtains, and I struggled
with these for a moment, but was finally defeated by
their mechanics and left the curtains closed.

In the middle of the floor was a model's throne,
with a sheeted shape in the middle which proved to
be an ornate gilt chair. The mice had been at the seat
of this, too—scraps of red velvet and horsehair were
scattered about, along with mouse-droppings and a
great deal of dust.

Under another sheet I found Grenville's work-
bench; his brushes, his trays of paint-tubes, palettes,
knives, bottles of linseed oil, piles of unused canvases,
grimy with age. There was also a little collection of
objets trouvés, small things which, perhaps, had taken
his fancy. A sea-polished stone, half a dozen shells, a
bunch of gulls' feathers, probably collected for the
practical purpose of cleaning his pipe. There were
curling, faded snapshots, of nobody I recognized, a
blue and white Chinese ginger jar filled with pencils,
some bottles of fossilized Indian ink, a scrap of seal-
ing wax.

It was like prying, as though I were reading another person's diary. I put back the sheet and went

on to the true purpose of my visit, which was the stack of unframed canvases standing around the wall, each with its face turned inwards. These had been dust-covered too, but the sheets had slipped, draping themselves about the floor, and as I dislodged the first pile my fingers touched cobwebs, and a huge, disgusting spider went scuttling across the floor and lost itself in the shadows.

It was a slow business. Five or six at a time, I lifted out the pictures, dusted them off, leaned them in rows against the model's throne, shifting the rickety standard lamp so that the light should shine on them. Some were dated, but they were stacked away in no sort of chronological order, and for the most part I could tell neither when nor where they had been painted. I only knew that they compassed the whole of Grenville's professional life and all his interests.

There were landscapes, seascapes—the ocean in all its moods—charming interiors, some sketches of Paris, some that looked like Italy. There were boats and fishermen, street scenes of Porthkerris, a number of rough charcoal sketches of two children, whom I knew were Roger and Lisa. There were no portraits.

I began to make my selection, setting aside the pictures which I found particularly engaging. By the time I had reached the final pile, there were half a dozen of them propped against the seat of a sagging couch, and I was dirty and cold, with grimy hands and cobwebs clinging to my clothes. With the good feeling of a task nearly completed I went to sort out

the last pile of canvases. There were three pen and
ink drawings, and a view of a harbour with yachts at
anchor. And then . . .

It was the last canvas and the biggest of all. It
needed two hands and all my efforts to lift it out of its
dark corner and turn it around to face the light. I
held it upright with one hand and stood back, and the
face of the girl leapt out to meet me, the dark, tip-
tilted eyes smiling with a vitality undimmed by the
dust of the years that passed. I saw the dark hair and
the bumpy cheekbones and the sensuous mouth, not
smiling, but seeming to tremble on the brink of
laughter. And she wore the same fragile white dress,
the dress that she had worn for the portrait that hung
over the fireplace in the drawing room at Boscarva.

Sophia.

Ever since my mother had mentioned her name
I had been fascinated by her. The frustrations of
never knowing what she looked like had only in-
creased my obsession. But now that I had found her
and we were face to face at last, I felt like Pandora. I
had opened the box and the secrets were out, and
there was no way in the world of packing them back
and locking the lid once more.

I knew that face. I had talked to it, argued with
it; seen it scowl and smile; seen the dark eyes narrowed in anger and glint with amusement.

It was Joss Gardner.

11

All at once I was bitterly cold. It was dark now and the studio was icy, but as well I could feel the blood drain from my face like water out of a basin; I could hear the laboured thumping of my own heart, and I started, violently, to shiver. My first instinct was to put the portrait back where I had found it, pile some other canvases on top of it and hide it, like a criminal trying to conceal a body, or something worse.

But in the end I reached for a chair and arranged it carefully, so that it supported Sophia's portrait like an easel, and then I backed away on shaking legs and carefully lowered myself on to the sagging seat of the aged sofa.

Sophia and Joss.

Sophia the enchanting, and the baffling Joss, whom I had finally learned was not to be trusted.

She went to London, she got married, she had a baby, I think, Pettifer had told me. Then in 1942 she was killed in the Blitz.

But he had not mentioned Joss. And yet Joss and Sophia were so obviously, inextricably linked.

And I thought of my desk, my mother's desk that she meant me to have, hidden away at the back of Joss's workshop.

And I heard Mollie's voice. *I don't know why Grenville's so taken with Joss. It's frightening. It's as though Joss were able to exert some hold over him.*

Sophia and Joss.

It was dark now. I had no watch and I had lost all track of time. The wind drowned all other sound, so that I did not hear Eliot coming down the garden from the house, picking his way through the darkness because I had taken the torch. I did not hear anything until the door burst open, as though on a gust of wind, causing the light to start up its demented swinging, and frightening me nearly out of my wits. The next instant Rufus bounded in and flung himself up on the sofa beside me, and I realized that I had company.

My cousin Eliot stood in the open doorway framed in darkness. He wore a suede jacket and a pale blue polo-necked sweater and he had slung a raincoat around his shoulders like a cloak. The cruel light drained all the colour from his thin face, and turned his deep-set eyes into two black holes.

"My mother told me you were down here. I came to . . ."

He stopped, and I knew that he had seen the portrait. I couldn't move, I was too petrified with cold, and anyway, now it was too late to do anything about it.

He came into the studio and closed the door. The leaping shadows, once more, were slowly stilled.

We neither of us said anything. I held Rufus's head, instinctively seeking comfort in his soft, warm fur, and watched while Eliot shrugged off his raincoat, dropped it across a chair, and came slowly to sit beside me. His eyes never left the portrait.

At last he spoke. "Good God," he said.

I said nothing.

"Where did you find that?"

"In a corner . . ." My voice came out as a croak. I cleared my throat and tried again. "In a corner, behind a lot of other canvases."

"It's Sophia."

"Yes."

"It's Joss Gardner."

There was no denying it. "Yes."

"Sophia's grandson, do you suppose?"

"Yes. I think he must be."

"Well, I'll be damned." He leaned back, and crossed his long, elegant legs, suddenly relaxed, like a knowledgeable art critic at a private view.

His obvious satisfaction puzzled me, and I did not want him to think that I shared it.

I said, "I wasn't looking for it. I've been wanting to know what Sophia looked like, but I had no idea there was a portrait of her down here. I just came to look for a picture because Grenville said I could have one to take back to London."

"I know. My mother told me."

"Eliot, we mustn't say anything."

He ignored this. "You know, there was always something funny about Joss, something unexplained. The way he turned up in Porthkerris, out of the blue. And the way Grenville knew that he was there; the way he gave him a job, and the run of Boscarva. I never trusted Joss farther than I could see him. And the desk disappearing—the desk that should have come to you. It was all fishy beyond words."

I knew that I should tell Eliot then that I had found the desk. I opened my mouth with the intention of doing just this thing, and closed it again because somehow the words would not be spoken. Besides, Eliot was still talking and had not noticed my incipient interruption.

"My mother swore he had some sort of a hold over Grenville."

"You make it sound like blackmail."

"Perhaps, in a modified form, it was. You know, 'Here I am Sophia's grandson, what are you going to do for me?' And Pettifer must have known as well. Pettifer and Grenville have no secrets from each other."

"Eliot, we mustn't say that we found the picture."

He turned his head to look at me.

"You sound anxious, Rebecca. On Joss Gardner's behalf?"

"No. On Grenville's."

"But you like Joss."

"No."

He pretended to be amazed. "But everybody likes Joss! Everybody, it seems, has fallen under his spell of boyish charm. Grenville and Pettifer; Andrea is besotted by him, she never leaves him alone, but I think there may be something just a little physical in that attraction. I thought that you were bound to have joined the club." He frowned. "You *did* like Joss."

"Not now, Eliot."

He began to be intrigued. He shifted his position slightly, so that we half-faced each other on the sofa, his arm along its carved back, behind my shoulder.

"What happened?" he asked.

What had happened? Nothing. But I had never felt quite easy about Joss, and all the coincidences that seemed to tie our lives together. And he had stolen my mother's desk. And he was now, at this moment, carrying on his clandestine affair with the unsavoury Andrea. At the very idea of this, my imagination was apt to turn and run.

Eliot was waiting for my reply. But I only shrugged and shook my head hopelessly and said, "I changed my mind."

"Could yesterday have had anything to do with it?"

"Yesterday?" I thought of sitting with Eliot on the sunbaked terrace of the little pub; of the two boys sailing their dinghy down the blue waters of the creek; and finally Eliot's arms, encircling and holding me, the feel of his kisses, and the sensation of losing control, of sliding over a cliff.

I shivered again. My hands, cold and grimy, lay in my lap. Eliot put his own over them and said, in some surprise, "You're freezing."

"I know, I've been here for hours."

"My mother told me you want to go back to London." We seemed to have dropped the subject of Joss and I was thankful for this.

"Yes, I have to go."

"When?"

"Tomorrow night."

"You never told me."

"I didn't decide until this morning."

"You seem to have changed your mind, and made a lot of decisions all in one day."

"I hadn't realized how the time had flown. I've been away from work for nearly two weeks."

"Yesterday, I asked you to stay."

"I have to go."

"What would make you stay?"

"Nothing. I mean . . . I can't . . ." I was stammering like a fool, but I was too cold, too dirty and too tired for such a conversation. Later, perhaps, I would be able to cope . . .

"Would you stay if I asked you to marry me?"

My head shot up. Something like horror must have shown on my face, for he put back his head and laughed.

"Don't look so shocked. There's nothing shocking about getting married."

"But we're cousins."

"That doesn't matter."

"But we don't . . . I mean . . . You don't love me."

It was an appalling thing to say, but Eliot took it in his stride.

"Rebecca, you are stammering and stuttering like a shy schoolgirl. Perhaps I do love you. Perhaps I would have loved you for a long time before asking you to marry me, but you've precipitated this situation by suddenly announcing out of the blue that you're going to go back to London. So if I'm going to say it at all, I'd better say it now. I want you to marry me. I think it would work very well."

Despite myself, I was touched. No one had ever asked me to marry them before, and I found it flattering. But even as I listened to Eliot with one part of my mind, the other part ran round in circles like a squirrel in a cage.

Because there was still Boscarva, and the land that Eliot needed to sell to Ernest Padlow.

You are not my only grandchild.

". . . it seems ridiculous to say goodbye and walk out of each other's lives when we've only just met each other, and there are so many good things going for us."

I said quietly, "Like Boscarva."

His smile froze slightly around the edges. He raised an eyebrow. "Boscarva?"

"Let's be honest and truthful, Eliot. For some

reason you need Boscarva. And you think that Grenville might leave it to me."

He took a deep breath as though to deny this, hesitated, and then let it all out in a long sigh. His smile was rueful. He ran a hand over the top of his head.

"How cool you are. The Ice Princess all of a sudden."

"You need Boscarva so that you can sell the farm to Ernest Padlow to build his houses."

He said, carefully, "Yes." I waited. "I needed money to build the garage. Grenville wasn't interested so I approached Padlow. He agreed and the security was the Boscarva farm. Gentleman's agreement."

"But it wasn't yours."

"I was sure it would be. There was no reason why it shouldn't be. And Grenville was old and ill. The end could have come any day." He spread his hands. "Who would have imagined that three years later he'd still be with us?"

"You sound as though you want him dead."

"Old age is a terrible thing. Lonely and sad. He's had a good life. What is there for him to cling on for?"

I knew that I could not agree with Eliot. Old age, in Grenville's case, meant dignity and purpose. I had only just got to know him, but already I loved him and he was part of me; I could not bear to think of him dying.

I said, trying to stay practical, "Isn't there some other way you could pay off Mr Padlow?"

"I could sell the garage. The way things are going I might have to do that anyway."

"I thought you were doing so well."

"That's what everybody's meant to think."

"But if you sold the garage, what would you do then?"

"What do you suggest I should do?" He sounded amused as though I were a child with whims to be indulged. I said, "How about Mr Kemback, and the car museum in Birmingham?"

"What an uncomfortably good memory you've got."

"Would working for Mr Kemback be such a bad thing?"

"And leave Cornwall?"

"I think that's what you should do. Make a new start. Get away from Boscarva and . . ." I stopped, and then thought, *in for a penny, in for a pound,* ". . . and your mother." I finished in a rush.

"My mother?" Still that amusement, as though I were a beguiling fool.

"You know what I mean, Eliot."

There was a long pause. Then, "I think," said Eliot, "you have been talking to Grenville."

"I'm sorry."

"One thing's for certain, either Joss or I will have to go. As they say in Westerns, 'This town ain't big enough for the two of us.' But I'd rather Joss went."

"Joss is unimportant. He's not worth taking a stand over."

"If I sold the garage and went to work in Birmingham, would you come with me?"

"Oh, Eliot . . ."

I turned away from him and came face to face once more with Sophia's portrait. Her eyes met mine and it was as though Joss sat there, listening to every word we were saying, laughing at us. Then Eliot put his hand beneath my chin and jerked my head around so that once more I was forced to meet his eye.

"Listen to what I'm saying!"

"I am listening."

"We don't have to be in love with each other. You know that, don't you?"

"I always imagined it was important."

"It doesn't happen to everyone. Perhaps it won't ever happen to you."

It was a chill prospect. "Perhaps not."

"In that case," his voice was very gentle and reasonable, "would a compromise be such a bad thing? Wouldn't a compromise be better than a nine to five job for the rest of your life and an empty flat in London?"

He had touched me on the raw. I had been alone for too long, and the prospect of staying alone for the rest of my life was frightening. Grenville had said, *You were made for a man and a home and children.* And now they were all there, waiting for me. I had only to reach out my hand, to accept what Eliot was offering me.

I said his name, and he put his arms around me, and drew me very close, kissing my eyes, my cheeks, my mouth. Sophia watched us and I did not care. I told myself that she was dead, and Joss I had already put out of my life. Why should I care what either of them thought of me?

Eliot said at last, "We must go." He held me away from him. "You must have a bath and wash all those dirty marks off your face, and I must get the ice out of the fridge, and be all ready and dutiful to pour drinks for Grenville and my mother."

"Yes." I drew away from his arms, and pushed a lock of hair out of my face. I felt deathly tired. "What time is it?"

He looked at his watch, the strap that I had given him still shining and new. "Nearly half past seven. We could stay here all night, but unfortunately life has to go on."

I got wearily to my feet. Without looking at the portrait I took it up and put it back in its hidden, dusty corner, along with the cobwebs and the spiders, its face to the wall. Then I picked up other pictures, at random, and piled them around and against it. Everything, I told myself, was just as it had been before. We tidied up in a cursory fashion and covered the canvases with the fallen dust-sheet. Eliot switched off the standard lamp, and I picked up the torch. We went out of the studio, turning off the light and closing and locking the door. Eliot took the torch from me, and together, following the bobbing circle of light, we went up the garden, stumbling a little over hidden verges and tussocks of grass, mounting the shining wet steps of the terrace. Above us the house loomed, lighted rooms glowing behind drawn curtains, and all around us was the wind and the silhouettes of leafless, tormented trees.

"I've never known a storm to last so long," said Eliot, as he opened the side door and we went inside. The hall felt warm and safe, and there was the good smell of the chicken casserole that we were to have for dinner.

We parted, Eliot heading for the kitchen, and I upstairs to shed my filthy clothes, draw a bath and wallow in warm, scented steam. Relaxed at last I thought about nothing. I was too tired to think. I would fall asleep, I decided, and probably drown. For some reason the idea of this did not alarm me.

But I did not fall asleep, because as I lay there, I heard, above the noise of the wind, the sound of an approaching car. The bathroom faced over the back of the house, the drive and the front door. I had not bothered to draw the curtains and the headlights of the car flashed for a second against the dark glass. A door banged, there were voices. Thus disturbed, I climbed out of the bath, dried myself and started across the passage to my room, but stopped dead when I heard the raised voices carrying up the stair-well from the hall.

". . . found her half way up the hill . . ." a man's voice, unrecognized.

And then Mollie, ". . . but my dear child . . ." This was interrupted by a wild cacophony of sobbing. I heard Eliot say, "For heaven's sake, girl . . ." And then Mollie again. "Come in by the fire . . . come along now, you're all right. You're safe now . . ."

I went into my room, pulled on my clothes, buttoned the neck of the brown caftan, brushed and plaited my hair, all in the space of moments. I painted on a layer of lipstick—there was no time for more—thrust my bare feet into sandals and ran downstairs, screwing on my ear-rings as I did so.

As I reached the bottom of the stairs Pettifer appeared through the kitchen door with a face like a thundercloud and bearing in his hand a glass of brandy. It was indicative of the gravity of the situation that he had omitted to put it on a silver salver.

"Pettifer, what's happened?"

"I don't know what's happened, exactly, but it sounds as though that girl's having hysterics."

"I heard a car coming. Who brought her home?"

"Morris Tatcombe. Says he was driving home from Porthkerris when he found her on the road."

I was horrified. "You mean *lying* on the road? Had she been hit by a car, or something?"

"I don't know. Probably just had a tumble."

At the far end of the hall the drawing room door burst open and Mollie came towards us, half running.

"Oh, Pettifer, don't stand talking, hurry with the brandy." She saw me standing, quite at a loss. "Oh, my dear Rebecca, what a terrible thing, quite terrible. I'm going to ring the doctor." She was at the telephone, thumbing through the book, unable to see because she had somewhere mislaid her glasses. "Look it up for me, there's a dear. It's Doctor Trevaskis . . . we ought to have it written down somewhere, but I can't find . . ."

Pettifer had gone. I took the telephone book and started to look for the number. "What's happened to Andrea?" I asked.

"It's the most ghastly story. I can hardly believe it's true. What a mercy Morris found her. She could have been there all night. She could have died . . ."

"Here it is. Lionel Trevaskis. Porthkerris 873."

She put a hand to her cheek. "Oh, of course, I should know it off by heart." She lifted the receiver and dialled. While she waited she spoke to me, swiftly. "Go and sit by her, the men are so useless, they never know what to do."

Mystified and oddly reluctant to know the details of Andrea's unhappy experience, I nevertheless did as she asked me. I found the drawing room in something approaching a shambles. Grenville, apparently nonplussed, stood in front of the fireplace with his hands behind his back and said nothing. The rest of them were grouped around the sofa; Eliot had given Morris a drink, and they watched while Pettifer, with commendable patience, was trying to trickle some brandy down Andrea's throat.

And Andrea . . . despite myself I was shocked and frightened by her appearance. The neat sweater and the pressed jeans in which she had set out so gaily were soaking wet and smeared with mud. Through the tear in the jeans I could see her knee, cut and bleeding, vulnerably childlike. She had lost, it seemed, a shoe. Her hair clung, like seaweed, to her skull, her face was blotched with crying, and when I said her name she turned her head to look at me from pathetic, streaming eyes; I saw with horror the great bruise on her temple, as though she had been savagely struck. The Celtic cross on its leather thong was also lost; torn off, perhaps, in some unthinkable struggle.

"Andrea!"

She gave a great wail and heaved herself over to press her face into the back of the sofa, spilling the brandy as she did so, and knocking the tumbler clean out of Pettifer's hand.

"I don't want to talk about it. I don't want to talk about it . . . !"

"But you must!"

Pettifer, exasperated, collected the glass and went from the room. I told myself that he had never liked the girl. I took his place beside her, sitting on the edge of the sofa, trying to turn her shoulders toward me.

"Did somebody do this to you?"

Andrea flung herself back at me, her body convulsed. "Yes!" She screamed at my face as though

I were deaf. "Joss!" And with that she dissolved once more in a welter of sobs.

I looked up at Grenville and was subjected to a stony, unblinking glare. His features might have been carved from wood. I decided there was no help to be expected from that quarter. I turned to Morris Tatcombe.

"Where did you find her?"

He shifted, one foot to another. I saw that he was dressed as though for a night on the town. A leather jacket, decorated with a rash of embroidered emblems, and spotted with rain, skin-tight jeans and boots with high heels. Even with high heels the top of his head scarcely reached to Eliot's shoulder, and his long hair hung damp and lank.

He tossed this back, a gesture both aggressive and self-conscious.

"Half way up Porthkerris Hill. You know, where the road narrows and there isn't a pavement. She was half way up the bank, half in the ditch. Lucky I saw her, really. Thought she'd been hit by a car, but it wasn't that. Seems she had this row with Joss Gardner."

I said, "He asked her to go to the cinema with him."

"I don't know how it all started," said Morris.

"But this, it seems—" said Eliot gravely— "is how it ends."

"But . . ." There had to be some other explanation. I was about to tell them this when Andrea let out another wail, like some aged sibyl keening at a wake, and I lost my temper.

"Oh, for goodness sake, girl, shut up!" I took her by her shoulders and gave her a little shake so that her head bobbed on the silk cushion like a badly stuffed rag-doll. "Stop making that dementing noise and tell us what happened."

Words began to spill out of her mouth, made ugly with weeping. (I thought briskly, *at least she isn't missing any teeth,* and hated myself for my own hard heart.)

"I . . . we . . . went to the cinema . . . and wh . . . when we came out, we went to a pub, and . . ."

"Which pub?"

"I don't know . . ."

"You must know which pub . . ."

My voice rose in impatience. Behind me, Mollie, whom I had not heard come into the room, said, "Oh, don't shout at her. Don't be unkind."

I made an effort and tried again, more gently.

"Can't you remember where you went?"

"No. It was d . . . dark . . . and I . . . couldn't see. And then . . . and then . . ."

I held her firmly, trying to calm her "Yes. And then?"

"And Joss had a lot of whisky to drink. And he wouldn't bring me home. He wanted me to g . . . go back to his flat with him . . . and . . ."

Her mouth went square, her features dissolved into uncontrollable weeping. I let her go and stood up, backing away from her. At once Mollie took my place.

"There," she said. "There, there." She was more gentle than I, her voice as soothing as a mother's. "Now there's nothing more to worry about. The doctor's on his way, and Pettifer's putting a nice hot bottle in your bed. You don't need to tell us any more. You don't need to talk about it any more."

But, perhaps calmed by Mollie's manner, Andrea seemed anxious to make a clean breast of it, and, through interminable sobs and gasps, we were to hear the rest of the story.

"And I didn't want to go. I . . . I wanted to come home. And I . . . left him. And he came after me. And . . . I tried to run, and I tripped on the p . . . pavement, and my shoe . . . c . . . came off. And then he c . . . caught me, and he be . . . began shouting at me . . . and I screamed and he *hit* me . . ."

I looked at the faces around me, and the same horror and consternation, in varying degrees, was mirrored upon them. Only Grenville appeared coldly, deeply angry, but still he did not move, he did not say a word.

"It's all right," Mollie said again, her voice shaking only a little. "Now, everything's all right. Come along, upstairs."

Somehow Andrea, wilted and bedraggled, was eased off the sofa, but her legs would not hold her weight, and she started to collapse. It was Morris who, standing nearest to her, stepped forward and caught her before she fell, swinging her up, with surprising strength, into his puny arms.

"There," said Mollie, "Morris will carry you upstairs. You'll be all right . . ." She moved towards the door. "If you'll come this way, Morris."

"OK," said Morris, who did not appear to have much option in the matter.

I watched Andrea's face. As Morris moved, her eyes opened and looked straight into mine, and our glances clashed and held. And I knew that she was lying. And she knew that I knew she was lying.

Leaning her head against Morris's chest, she began to cry again. Swiftly, she was borne from the room.

We listened as Morris's burdened footsteps went down the hall, started up the staircase. Then Eliot said, with masterly understatement, "An unsavoury business." He glanced at Grenville. "Shall I ring the police now or later?"

Grenville spoke at last. "Who said anything about ringing the police?"

"You surely don't intend to let him get away with it?"

I said, "She was lying."

Both men looked at me in some surprise. Grenville's eyes narrowed and he was at his most formidable. Eliot frowned. "What did you say?"

"Some of her story may be true. Most of it probably is. But still, she was lying."

"How was she lying?"

"Because as you said yourself, she was besotted

with Joss. She wouldn't leave him alone. She told me that she'd been often to his flat, and she must have been, because she described it to me and every detail was right. I don't know what happened this evening. But I do know that if Joss wanted her to go back with him, she'd have gone like a shot. No arguments."

"Then how," asked Eliot smoothly, "do you account for the bruise on her face?"

"I don't know. I said I don't know about the rest of her story. But that bit, for sure, she made up."

Grenville moved. He had been standing for a long time. Slowly, he went to his chair and lowered himself carefully into it.

"We can find out what really happened," he said at last.

"How?" Eliot's question came out like the shot of a gun.

Grenville swung his head around and fixed his gaze on Eliot.

"We can ask Joss."

Eliot let out a sound, which in old-fashioned novels would have been written as "Pshaw."

"We shall ask him. And we will be given the truth."

"He doesn't know what the truth means."

"You have no justification for making such a statement."

Eliot lost his temper. "Oh, for God's sake, does the truth have to be thrown in your face before you recognize it?"

"Don't raise your voice to me."

Eliot was silent, staring in disbelief and disgust at the old man. When at last he spoke, it was in scarcely more than a whisper. "I've had enough of Joss Gardner. I've never trusted him nor liked him. I believe he's a phoney, a thief and a liar, and I know that I'm right. And one day you too will know that I'm right. This is your house. I accept that. But what I will not accept is his right to take it over, and us with it, just because he happens to be . . ."

I had to stop him. "Eliot!" He turned to look at me. It was as though he had forgotten I was there. "Eliot, please. Don't say any more."

He looked down at his glass, finished the drink in a single mouthful. "All right," he said at last. "For the moment, I won't say any more."

And he went to pour himself another whisky. As he did this, with Grenville and I watching him in silence, Morris Tatcombe came back into the room.

"I'll be off then," he said to the back of Eliot's head.

Eliot turned and saw him. "Is she all right?"

"Well, she's upstairs. Your mother's with her."

"Have another drink before you go."

"No, I'd better be off."

"We really can't thank you enough. What would have happened if you hadn't seen her . . ." He stopped, the unfinished sentence conjuring up visions of Andrea dying of exposure, exhaustion, loss of blood.

"Just lucky I did." He backed away, obviously anxious to be off, but not quite sure how to get there.

Eliot put the stopper into the decanter, left his freshly filled glass on the table and came to his rescue.

"I'll see you to the door."

Morris ducked his head in the general direction of Grenville and myself.

"Night, all."

But Grenville had hauled himself to his feet with massive dignity. "You've handled things very sensibly, Mr Tatcombe. We're grateful to you. And we would be grateful, too, if you would keep the girl's version of what happened to yourself. At least until it has been authenticated."

Morris looked sceptical. "These things get around."

"But not, I am sure, through you."

Morris shrugged. "It's your affair."

"Exactly. Our affair. Good night, Mr Tatcombe."

Eliot led him away.

Grenville laboriously settled himself once more in his chair. He passed a hand over his eyes, and it occurred to me that such scenes could not be good for him.

"Are you all right?"

"Yes. I'm all right."

I wished that I could confide in him, tell him that I knew about Sophia, and Joss being her grandson. But I knew that if there were any telling to be done, it had to come from him.

"Would you like a drink?"

"No."

So I left him alone, busying myself in tidying the cushions on the flattened sofa.

It was some time before Eliot re-appeared, but when he did he seemed quite cheerful again, the sudden row which had flared between him and Grenville now quite forgotten. He went to pick up his drink. "Good health," he said, raising his glass to his grandfather.

"I suppose we're in debt to that young man," said Grenville. "I hope one day we'll be able to settle it."

"I shouldn't worry too much about Morris," Eliot replied lightly. "I should think he's quite capable of settling it for himself. And Pettifer has asked me to tell you both that dinner is ready."

We ate alone, the three of us. Mollie stayed with Andrea, and in the middle of dinner the doctor arrived and was taken upstairs by Pettifer. Later, we heard him talking to Mollie in the hall, then she showed him out and came into the dining room to tell us what he had said.

"Shock, of course. He's given her a sedative, and she has to stay in bed for a day or two."

Eliot had gone to pull out a chair for her, and she sank into this looking exhausted and shaken. "Imagine such a thing happening. How I'm going to tell her mother, I can't think."

"Don't think about it," said Eliot, "till tomorrow."

"But it was such an appalling story. She's only a child. She's only seventeen. What could Joss have been thinking of? He must have gone out of his mind."

"He was probably drunk," said Eliot.

"Yes, perhaps he was. Drunk and violent."

Neither Grenville nor I said anything. It was as though we had entered into some sort of an unspoken conspiracy, but this did not mean that I had forgiven Joss, nor condoned anything that he had done. Later, probably, when he had been interrogated by Grenville, the whole truth would come out. By then I would probably be back in London.

And if I was still here . . . Slowly, I ate a little bunch of grapes. This could be my last dinner at Boscarva, but I truly did not know whether I wanted it to be or not. I had reached a cross-roads, and had no idea which was the way I should take. But soon I was going to have to make up my mind.

A compromise, Eliot had said, and it had sounded tepid. But after the histrionics of this evening, the very words had a solid ring to them, sensible and matter-of-fact, with their feet planted squarely on the ground.

You were made for a man and a home and children.

I reached for my wine glass and, glancing up, saw that Eliot watched me across the polished table. He smiled, as though we were conspirators. The expression on his face was both confident and triumphant. Perhaps, while I was thinking that I would probably end up by marrying him, he already knew that I would.

We were back in the drawing room, sitting around the fire and finishing our coffee, when the telephone started to ring. I thought that Eliot would go to answer it, but he was deep in a chair with the paper and a drink, and managed to linger so long that it was Pettifer who finally took the call. We heard the kitchen door open and his old feet go so slowly across the hall. The ringing stopped. For some reason I glanced up at the clock on the mantelpiece. It was nearly a quarter to ten.

We waited. Presently the door opened and Pettifer's head came around the edge of it, his spectacles glinting in the lamplight.

"Who is it, Pettifer?" asked Mollie.

"It's for Rebecca," said Pettifer.

I was surprised. "For me?"

Eliot said, "Who's ringing you at this hour of the day?"

"I've no idea."

I got up and went out of the room. Perhaps it was Maggie, wanting to tell me something about the flat. Perhaps it was Stephen Forbes, wondering when I was going to return to work. I felt guilty, because I should have been in touch with him, letting him know what I was doing and when I planned to go back to London.

I sat on the hall chest and picked up the receiver.

"Hallo?"

A small, mouse-like voice began speaking, sounding very far away.

"Oh, Miss Bayliss, we were passing, and he was lying there . . . my husband said . . . so we got him up the stairs and into the flat . . . don't know what happened. Covered in blood and he could hardly talk. Wanted to call the doctor . . . but he wouldn't let us . . . frightened leaving him there on his own . . . there ought to be somebody there . . . said he'd be all right . . ."

I must have been exceptionally slow and stupid, but it took me a little time to realize that this was Mrs Kernow, calling me from the phone box at the end of Fish Lane, to tell me that something had happened to Joss.

12

~~~

I was amazed and gratified to find myself in a state of almost total calm. It was as though I had already been prepared for this crisis, been given my orders and told what to do. There were no doubts and so no indecision. I must go to Joss. It was as simple as that.

I went up to my bedroom and got my coat, put it on, did up the buttons, came downstairs again. The key of Mollie's car lay where I had left it, on the brass tray in the middle of the table in the hall.

I picked it up, and as I did so the drawing room door opened and Eliot came up the passage towards me. It never occurred to me that he would try to stop me going. It never occurred to me that anyone or anything could stop me going.

He saw me, bundled into my old leather coat. "Where are you off to?"

"Out."

"Who was that on the telephone?"

"Mrs. Kernow."

"What does she want?"

"Joss has been hurt. She and Mr Kernow were walking home along the harbour road, they'd been visiting her sister. They found him."

"So?" His voice was cold and very quiet. I expected to be intimidated, but I was not.

"I'm going to borrow your mother's car. I'm going to him."

His thin face hardened, the skin drawn tight over the jutting bones.

"Have you gone out of your mind?"

"I don't think so."

He said nothing. I slipped the key into my pocket and made for the door, but Eliot was faster than I, and in two strides was in front of me, standing with his back to the door and with his hand on the latch.

"You're not going," he said pleasantly. "You don't really think I'd let you go?"

"He's been hurt, Eliot."

"So what? You saw what he did to Andrea. He's rotten, Rebecca. You know he's rotten. His grandmother was an Irish whore, God knows who his father was, and he's a womanizing bastard."

The ugly words, which were meant to shock me, slid off my back like water from a duck. Eliot saw this and my unconcern infuriated him.

"Why do you want to go to him? What good could you do? He won't thank you for interfering, if it's thanks you're looking for. Leave him alone, he has no part of your life, he's none of your concern."

I stood watching him, hearing him, without

making sense of anything he said. But I knew, all at once, that it was over, the uncertainty and the indecision, and I felt light with relief, as though a great weight had been lifted from my shoulders. I still stood at the crossroads. My life was still a confusion. But one thing had made itself abundantly clear. I could never marry Eliot.

A compromise, he had said. But, for me, it would have been a poor bargain. All right, he was weak, and probably not the most successful of businessmen. I had recognized these flaws in his character and had been prepared to accept them. But the welcome he had shown me, the hospitality, and the charm which he could turn on and off like a tap, had blinded me to his vindictiveness and the frightening strength of his jealousy.

I said, "Let me go, Eliot."

"Supposing I say that I won't let you go? Supposing I keep you here?" He put his hands on either side of my head, pressing so tightly that it felt as though my skull would crack open, like a nut. "Supposing, now, that I said I loved you?"

I was sickened by him. "You don't love anyone. Only Eliot Bayliss. There's no room for anyone else in your life."

"I thought we decided that it was you who didn't know how to love."

His grip tightened. My head began to pound and I closed my eyes, enduring the pain.

"When I do—" I told him through clenched teeth—"it won't be you."

"All right then, go . . ." He let me loose so suddenly that I nearly lost my balance. Savagely he turned the handle and flung the door open, and instantly the wind poured in, like some monstrous creature that had been waiting all evening to invade the house. Outside was the dark and the rain. Without another word, not stopping to look at Eliot, I ran past him and out into it, as though to some sanctuary.

I had still to get to the garage, to struggle with doors in the darkness, to find Mollie's little car. I was convinced that Eliot was just behind me, as frightening as an imagined bogy man, waiting to jump, to catch me, to stop me from getting away. I slammed the car door shut, and my hand shook so much I could scarcely get the ignition key fitted. The first time I turned it, the engine did not start. I heard myself whimpering as I pulled out the choke and tried again. This time the engine caught. I put the car into gear and shot forward, through the darkness and the rain, up the puddled driveway with a great spattering of gravel, and so at last out and on to the road.

Driving, I regained some of my previous calm. I had eluded Eliot, I was going to Joss. I must drive with care and good sense, not allow myself to panic, not risk a skid or a possible collision. I slowed down to a cautious thirty miles per hour. I deliberately loosened my death-like clutch on the driving wheel. The road ran downhill, black and wet with rain. The lights of Porthkerris came up towards me. I was going to Joss.

Now, the tide was at full ebb. As I came out on to the harbour road, I saw the lights reflected in wet sand, the boats drawn up out of the reach of the storm. Overhead tattered scraps of cloud still poured across the sky. There were people about, but not very many.

The shop was in darkness. Only a single light glowed from the top window. I parked the car by the pavement and got out and went to the door and it opened. I smelt the new wood, my feet brushed through the shavings which still lay about the place. From the light of the street lamp outside I could see the staircase. I went up it, cautiously, to the first floor.

I called up, "Joss!"

There was no reply. I went on, up into the soft light. There was no fire and it was very cold. A squall of rain swept the roof above me.

"Joss."

He was lying on his bed, roughly covered by a blanket. His forearm lay across his eyes, as though to shut out some unbearable light. When I spoke he lowered this, and raised his head slightly to see who it was. Then he dropped back on to the pillow.

"Good God," I heard him say. "Rebecca."

I went to his side. "Yes, it's me."

"I thought I heard your voice. I thought I was dreaming."

"I called up, but you didn't reply."

His face was in a terrible mess, the left side bruised and swollen, the eye half-closed. Blood had trickled and dried from a cut in his lip, and there did not seem to be any skin on the knuckles of his right hand.

"What are you doing here?" He spoke muzzily, perhaps because of the lip.

"Mrs Kernow rang me."

"I told her not to say anything."

"She was worried about you. Joss, what happened?"

"I fell amongst thieves."

"Are you hurt anywhere else?"

"Yes, everywhere else."

"Let me see . . ."

"The Kernows bandaged me up."

But I stooped over him, gently drawing back the blanket. As far as his rib-cage he was naked and below this tenderly swathed in what looked like strips torn from an old sheet. But the ugly bruising had spread up and on to his chest, and on his right side the red stain of blood had started to seep through the white cotton.

"Joss, who did this?"

But Joss did not answer me. Instead, with a strength surprising in one so hurt, he put up an arm and pulled me down so that I was sitting on the edge of his bed. My long, blonde plait of hair hung forward over my shoulder, and while he held me with his right arm, his left hand was occupied in slipping off the rubber band which held the ends together, and then, using his fingers like a comb, he loosened the strands, unravelling them, so that my hair hung like a silken tassel, brushing on to his naked chest.

He said, "I always wanted to do that. Ever since I first saw you looking like the head girl of . . . what was it I said?"

"The head girl of a nicely run orphanage."

"That's it. Fancy you remembering."

"What can I do? There must be something I can do?"

"Just stay. Just stay, my darling girl."

The tenderness in his voice . . . Joss, who had always been so tough . . . dissolved me. Tears sprang into my eyes and he saw these and pulled me down, so that I lay against him, and I felt his hand slip up beneath my hair and close around the back of my neck.

"Joss, I'll hurt you . . ."

"Don't talk," he said, as his seeking mouth found mine. And then, "I've always wanted to do this, too."

It was evident that none of his infirmities, his bruises, his bleeding, his cut lip, were to deter him in any way from getting exactly what he wanted.

And I, who had always imagined that loving was something to do with fireworks and explosions of emotion, discovered that it was not like that at all. It was warm, like sudden sunshine. It had nothing to do with my mother and the endless procession of men who had invaded her life. It was cynicism and preconceived ideas flying out of an open window. It was the last of my defences gone. It was Joss.

He said my name and he made it sound beautiful.

Much later, I lit a fire, piling on the driftwood so that the room was bright with flickering firelight. I would not let Joss move, so that he lay with his dark head propped on his arms, and I felt his eyes following every move I made.

I stood up, away from the fire. My hair fell loose on either side of my face, and my cheeks were warm from the fire. I felt soft with content.

Joss said, "We have to talk, don't we?"

"Yes."

"Get me a drink."

"What do you want?"

"Some whisky. It's in the galley, in the cupboard over the sink."

I went to find it, and two glasses. "Soda or water?"

"Soda. There's a bottle-opener hanging on a hook."

I found the opener and took the cap off the bottle. I did this clumsily and it fell to the floor, rolling in the maddening manner of such things into a dark corner. I went to retrieve it and my eye was caught by another small and shining object, lying half under the kickboard beneath the sink. I picked it up and it was Andrea's Celtic cross, the one that she had worn on a leather thong around her neck.

I kept it in my hand. I poured the drinks and

took them back to Joss. I handed him one, and knelt on the floor beside him.

I said, "This was under the sink," and showed him the cross.

His swollen eye made it difficult for him to focus. He squinted at it painfully.

"What the hell's that?"

"It's Andrea's."

He said, "Oh, to hell." And then, "Get me some more pillows, there's a good girl. I could never drink whisky lying down."

I gathered up a couple of cushions off the floor, and propped him against them. The action of sitting up was agony for him and he let out an involuntary groan.

"Are you all right?"

"Yes, of course I'm all right. Where did you find that thing?"

"I told you. On the floor."

"She came here this evening. She said she'd been to the cinema. I was working downstairs, trying to get the shelving finished. I told her I was busy, but she just came up here, as though I'd never said a word. I followed her up and told her to go home. But she wouldn't go. She said she wanted a drink, she wanted to talk . . . you know the sort of drivel."

"She's been here before."

"Yes, once. One morning. I was sorry for her and I gave her a cup of coffee. But this evening I was busy; I had no time for her and I wasn't sorry for her. I said I didn't want a drink. I told her to go home.

And then she said that she didn't want to go home, everybody hated her, nobody would talk to her, I was the only person she could talk to, I was the only person who understood."

"Perhaps you were."

"OK, so I was sorry for her. I used to let her come and get in my way when I was working at Boscarva, because there wasn't much else I could do about it, short of bodily throwing her out of the room."

"Did you do that this evening? Throw her out?"

"Not in so many words. But finally I'd had enough of her batty conversation and her totally unfounded belief that I was ready, willing and eager to jump into bed with her, and I lost my temper and told her so."

"What happened then?"

"What didn't happen? Screams, tears, accusations, routine hysteria. I was subjected to every sort of vilification. Face slapping, the lot. That was when I finally resorted to force, and I bundled her down the stairs and threw her raincoat and her beastly handbag after her."

"You didn't hurt her?"

"No, I didn't hurt her. But I think I frightened her, because she went then, like the hammers of hell. I heard her clattering down the stairs on those ghastly clogs she wears, and then I think she must have slipped because there was the most frightful thumping and bumping as she went down the last few stairs. I shouted down to make sure she was all right, but then I heard her running out of the shop and slamming the door behind her, so that I imagined she was."

"Could she have hit herself on anything? Bruised her face when she fell?"

"Yes, I suppose she could. There was a packing case full of china standing at the bottom of the stairs. She could have collided with that . . . Why do you ask anyway?"

I told him. When I had finished he let out a long, incredulous whistle. But he was angry too.

"The little bitch. I think she's a nymphomaniac, do you know that?"

"I've always thought so."

"She was always talking about some guy called Danus, going into the most gruesome of intimate details. And the bloody cheek of telling everyone that I had asked her to go to the cinema with me. I wouldn't ask her to empty a dustbin with me . . . What's happened to her now?"

"She's been put to bed. Mollie got the doctor."

"If he's worth his salt he'll have diagnosed self-induced hysteria. And he'll prescribe a good walloping and send her back to London. And that'll get her out of everybody's way."

"Poor Andrea. She's very unhappy."

As though he could not keep his hands off it, he reached out to touch my hair. I turned my head and kissed the back of his hand, the lacerated knuckles.

He said, "You didn't believe her, did you?"

"Not really."

"Did anyone else?"

"Mollie and Eliot did. Eliot wanted to call the police but Grenville wouldn't let him."

"That's interesting."

"Why?"

"Who was it who brought Andrea home?"

"I thought I'd told you. Morris Tatcombe . . . you know, the boy who works for Eliot . . ."

"Morris? Well I'll be . . ." He stopped in mid-sentence, and then said again, "Morris Tatcombe."

"What about him?"

"Oh, Rebecca, come along. Pull yourself together. Use your wits. Who do you think gave me this beating?"

"Not Morris." I did not want to believe it.

"Morris and three others. I went along to The Anchor for a glass of beer and a pie for my supper, and when I was walking home, they jumped me."

"You knew it was Morris?"

"Who else would it be? He's always had this grudge going for me ever since we last crossed swords and he ended up on his backside in the gutter. I thought his putting the boot in this time was just a continuation of our running feud. But it seems that it wasn't."

Without thinking I began to say, "Eliot . . ." and then stopped, but it was too late. Joss said quietly, "What about Eliot?"

"I don't want to talk about Eliot."

"Did he tell Morris to come after me?"

"I don't know."

"He could, you know. He hates my guts. It fits."

"I . . . I think he's jealous of you. He doesn't like your being so close to Grenville. He doesn't like Grenville being so fond of you. And . . ." I looked down at my drink, turning the glass in my hand, feeling suddenly nervous. "There's something else."

"From your expression one would think you'd murdered somebody. What is it?"

"It's . . . the desk. The desk downstairs in your workroom. I saw it this morning, when you were telephoning."

"I wondered why you'd suddenly gone cantering out into the rain. What about it?"

"The desk and the Chippendale chair. They come from Boscarva."

"Yes, I know."

His calmness shocked me. "You didn't *take* them, Joss?"

"Take them? No, I didn't take them. I bought them."

"Who from?"

"A man who runs an antique shop up beyond Fourbourne. I'd been to a sale about a month ago, and I dropped in to see him on the way back, and I saw the chair and the desk in his shop. By then I knew all Grenville's furniture and I knew they'd come from Boscarva."

"But who took them?"

"I regret to have to shatter your innocence, but it was your cousin Eliot."

"But Eliot knew nothing about them."

"Eliot most certainly did. They were in one of the attics, as far as I remember, and he probably imagined they'd never be missed."

"But why . . . ?"

"This is like playing the truth game. Because Eliot, my love, my darling child, is head over heels in debt. That garage was financed by Ernest Padlow in the first place, it cost a bomb and it's been losing money steadily for the past twelve months. God knows what use fifty pounds would have been to Eliot, a mere drop in the ocean one would have thought, but perhaps he needed a little ready cash to pay a bill or put on a horse or something . . . I don't know. Between you and me, I don't think he should be running his own business. He'd be better working for some other guy, being paid a regular salary. Perhaps, one evening, when you're sitting over drinks at Boscarva, you could try and persuade him."

"Sarcasm doesn't suit you."

"I know, but Eliot makes me edgy. Always has done."

I felt, obscurely, that I must stand up for Eliot, make excuses for him.

"In a way, he thinks that Boscarva and everything in it already belong to him. Perhaps he didn't feel it was . . . stealing . . . ?"

"When did they realize the things were missing?"

"A couple of days ago. You see, the desk belonged to my mother. Now it belongs to me. That's why we started to look for it."

"Unfortunate for Eliot."

"Yes."

"I suppose Eliot said I'd taken them."

"Yes," I admitted miserably.

"What did Grenville say?"

"He said that you'd never do a thing like that."

"And so there was another monumental row."

"Yes."

Joss sighed deeply. We fell silent. The room was growing cold again, the fire beginning to die down. I got up and went to put another log on it, but Joss stopped me.

"Leave it," he said.

I looked at him, surprised. He finished his drink and put the empty glass down on the floor beside him, and then pushed back the blanket and began, carefully, to get out of bed.

"Joss, you mustn't . . ."

I flew to his side, but he pushed me away, and slowly, with infinite caution, got to his feet. Once there, he grinned triumphantly down at me, a bizarre sight, bruised and battered, and dressed in bandages and a crumpled pair of jeans.

"Into battle," he said.

"Joss, what are you going to do?"

"If you'll find me a shirt and a pair of shoes, I'll get dressed. And then we're going to go downstairs, and get into the truck and drive back to Boscarva."

"But you can't drive like that."

"I can do anything I want," he told me, and I

believed him. "Now find my clothes and stop arguing."

He would not even let me take Mollie's car. "We'll leave it there, it'll be all right. Someone can fetch it in the morning." His own little truck was parked around the corner, up a narrow alley. We got in, and he started the engine and backed out on to the road, with me giving directions because he was too stiff to turn around in the seat. We headed up through the town, along streets that had become familiar to me, over the cross-roads and up the hill.

I sat, staring ahead, with my hands clasped tightly in my lap. I knew that there was still something else we had to talk about. And it had to be now, before we reached Boscarva.

For some reason, as though he were immensely pleased with life in general, Joss has started to sing.

"The first time ever I saw your face
I thought the sun rose in your eyes
And the moon and stars . . ."

"Joss."

"What is it now?"

"There's something else."

He sounded shocked. "Not another skeleton in the cupboard?"

"Don't joke."

"I'm sorry. What is it?"

I swallowed a strange obstruction in the back of my throat.

"It's Sophia."

"What about Sophia?"

"Grenville gave me the key of the studio so that I could go and choose a picture to take back to London. I found a portrait of Sophia. A proper one, with a face. And Eliot came to find me, and he saw it too."

There was a long silence. I looked at Joss but his profile was stony, intent on the road ahead. "I see," he said at last.

"She looks just like you; or you look just like her."

"Naturally enough. She was my grandmother."

"Yes, I thought that was probably it."

"So the portrait was in the studio?"

"Is . . . is that why you came to live in Porthkerris?"

"Yes. Grenville and my father fixed it between them. Grenville put up half the capital for my shop."

"Your father . . . ?"

"You've met him. Tristram Nolan Gardner. He runs an antique shop, in the New Kings Road. You bought a pair of balloon-back chairs from him. Do you remember?"

"And he found from my cheque that I was called Rebecca Bayliss."

"Right. And he found out, by cunning question and answer, that you were Grenville Bayliss's granddaughter. Right. And he found out that you were catching the train to Cornwall last Monday. Right."

"So he rang you up and told you to meet the train."

"Right."

"But why?"

"Because he felt involved. Because he thought you seemed lost and vulnerable. Because he wanted me to keep an eye on you."

"I still don't understand."

"You know something?" said Joss. "I love you very much."

"Because I'm being stupid?"

"No, because you're being marvellously innocent. Sophia wasn't only Grenville's model, she was his mistress as well. My father was born at the beginning of their relationship, long before your mother arrived. Sophia married, eventually, an old friend she'd known from childhood days, but she never had any more children."

"So Tristram . . . ?"

"Tristram is Grenville's son. And Grenville is my grandfather. And I am going to marry my half-cousin."

"Pettifer told me that Sophia meant nothing to Grenville. That she was just a girl who'd worked for him."

"If it meant protecting Grenville, Pettifer would swear that black is white."

"Yes, I suppose he would." But Grenville, in anger, had been less discreet. " 'You are not my only grandchild!' "

"Did Grenville say that?"

"Yes, to Eliot. And Eliot thought he meant me."

We had reached the top of the hill. The lights of

the town were far behind us. Ahead, beyond the huddled shapes of Ernest Padlow's housing estate, lay the dark coastline, pricked with the tiny lights of random farms, and beyond it the black immensity of the sea.

I said, "I don't seem to remember you asking me to marry you."

The little van bumped and lurched down the lane towards Boscarva. "I'm not very good at asking things," said Joss. He took his hand off the wheel and put it over mine. "I usually just tell people."

As once before, it was Pettifer who came out to meet us. As soon as Joss switched off the engine of the van, the light in the hall went on, and Pettifer opened the door, as though he had known instinctively we were on our way.

He saw Joss open the car door and ease himself out, in obvious discomfort and pain. He saw Joss's face . . .

"For heaven's sake, what happened to you?"

"I had a difference of opinion with our old friend Morris Tatcombe. I probably wouldn't look like this except that he had three of his chums with him."

"Are you all right?"

"Yes, I'm fine. No bones broken. Come on, let's go in."

We went indoors and Pettifer closed the door.

"I'm glad to see you, Joss, and that's the truth. We've had a proper how-do-you-do here and no mistake."

"Is Grenville all right?"

"Yes, he's all right. He's still up, in the drawing room, waiting for Rebecca to come home."

"And Eliot?"

Pettifer looked from Joss's face to mine.

"He's gone."

Joss said, "You'd better tell us about it."

We ended up in the kitchen, around the table.

"After Rebecca had gone, Eliot went down to the studio and came back with that portrait of Sophia. The one we looked for, Joss. The one we never found."

I said, "I don't understand."

Joss explained. "Pettifer knew Sophia was my grandmother, but no one else did. No one else remembered her. It was all too long ago. Grenville wanted it to stay that way."

"But why was there only one picture of Sophia with a face? There must have been dozens Grenville painted of her. What happened to all of them?"

There was a pause while Joss and Pettifer looked at each other. Then it was Pettifer's turn to explain, which he did with much tact.

"It was old Mrs Bayliss. She was jealous of Sophia . . . not because she had any notion of the truth . . . but because Sophia was part of the Commander's other life, the life Mrs Bayliss didn't have no time for."

"You mean his painting."

"She would never have anything to do with Sophia, more than a frosty good morning if she happened to meet her in the town. And the Commander knew this, and he didn't want to upset her, so he let all the pictures of Sophia go . . . all except for the one you found. We knew it was somewhere around. Joss and I spent a day looking for it, but we never turned it up."

"What were you going to do with it if you found it?"

"Nothing. We just didn't want anyone else to find it."

"I don't see why it was so important."

Joss said, "Grenville didn't want anyone to know about what happened between him and Sophia. It wasn't that he was ashamed of it, because he'd loved her very much. And after he's dead, it won't matter any longer, he doesn't give a damn who knows then. But he's proud, and he's lived his life according to a certain set of standards. We probably think they're old-fashioned, but they're still his own. Does that make sense to you?"

"I suppose so."

"Young people now," said Pettifer heavily, "talk about a permissive society as though it were something they'd invented. But it's not new. It's been going on since the beginning of time, only in the Commander's day it was handled with a little more discretion."

We accepted this meekly. Then Joss said, "We seem to have gone off at a tangent. Pettifer was telling us about Eliot."

Pettifer collected himself. "Yes, well. So down to

the drawing room Eliot went, and stormed in, with me behind him, went straight to the mantelpiece, and dumped it up there, alongside the other picture. The Commander never said a word, just watched him. And Eliot said, 'What's that got to do with Joss Gardner?' Then the Commander told him. Told him everything. Very quiet and very dignified. And Mrs Roger was there too, and she just about threw a fit. She said all these years the Commander had deceived them, letting Eliot believe that he was his only grandson, and he'd get Boscarva when the Commander died. The Commander said he'd never said anything of the sort, that it was all surmise, that they'd simply been counting their chickens before they were hatched. Then Eliot said, very cold, 'Perhaps now we can know what your plans are?' but the Commander said that his plans were his own business, and *quite right* he was too."

This little bit of championship was accompanied by Pettifer's fist coming down with a thump on the kitchen table.

"So what did Eliot do?"

"Eliot said in that case he was going to wash his hands of the whole lot of us . . . meaning the family, of course . . . and that he had plans of his own and he was thankful to be shed of us. And with that he collected a few papers and a brief-case and put on his coat and whistled up his dog and walked out of the house. Heard his car go up the lane and that was the end of him."

"Where's he gone?"

"To High Cross, I suppose."

"And Mollie?"

"She was in tears . . . trying to stop him doing anything stupid, she said. Begging him to stay. Turning on the Commander, saying it was all his fault. But of course, there wasn't anything she could do to stop Eliot. There's nothing you can do to stop a grown man walking out of the house, not even if you do happen to be his mother."

I was torn with sorrow and sympathy for Mollie. "Where is she now?"

"Up in her room." He added gruffly, "I made her a little tea tray, took it up to her, found her sitting at her dressing-table like something carved out of stone."

I was glad I had not been here. It all sounded very dramatic. I stood up. Poor Mollie. "I'll go up and talk to her."

"And I—" said Joss—"will go and see Grenville."

"Tell him I'll be there in a moment or two."

Joss smiled. "We'll wait," he promised.

I found Mollie, white-faced and tear-stained, still sitting in front of her frilled dressing-table. (This was in character. Even the deepest excesses of grief would not cause Mollie to fling herself across any bed. It might crease the covers.) As I came into the room, she looked up, and her reflection was caught three times over in her triple mirror; for the first time ever, I thought that she looked her age.

I said, "Are you all right?"

She looked down, balling a sodden handkerchief in her fingers. I went to her side. "Pettifer told me. I'm so very sorry."

"It's all so desperately unfair. Grenville's always disliked Eliot, resented him in some extraordinary way. And of course, now we know why. He was always trying to run Eliot's life, come between Eliot and me. Whatever I did for Eliot was always wrong."

I knelt beside her, and put my arm around her, "I really believe he meant it for the best. Can't you try to believe that too?"

"I don't even know where he's gone. He wouldn't tell me. He never said goodbye."

I realized that she was a great deal more worried about Eliot's abrupt departure than she was about the evening's revelations concerning Joss. This was just as well. I could comfort her about Eliot. There was not a mortal thing I could do about Joss.

"I think," I said, "that Eliot may have gone to Birmingham."

She looked at me in horror. *"Birmingham?"*

"There was a man there who wanted to give him a job. Eliot told me. It was to do with second-hand cars. He seemed to think that it might be quite interesting."

"But I can't go and live in *Birmingham.*"

"Oh, Mollie, you don't have to. Eliot can live on his own. Let him go. Give him the chance of making something of his life."

"But we've always been together."

"Then perhaps it's time to start living apart.

You've got your house at High Cross, your garden up there, your friends . . ."

"I can't leave Boscarva. I can't leave Andrea. I can't leave Grenville."

"Yes, you can. And I think Andrea should go back to London, to her own parents. You've done all you can for her, and she's miserable here. That's why all this happened, because she was unhappy and lonely. And as for Grenville, I'll stay with him."

I came downstairs at last, carrying the tea tray. I took it into the kitchen and put it on the table. Pettifer, sitting there, looked up at me over the edge of his evening paper.

"How is she?" he asked.

"All right now. She's agreed that Andrea should go home, back to London. And then she's going back to High Cross."

"That's what she's always wanted. And you?"

"I'm staying here. If that's all right with you."

A chill gleam of satisfaction crossed Pettifer's face, the nearest he could get to a look of delight. There was no need for me to say more. We understood each other.

Pettifer turned his paper. "They're in the drawing room—" he told me—"waiting for you," and he settled down to the racing page.

I went and found them, backed by the two portraits of Sophia in her white dress, Joss standing by the fire, and Grenville deep in his chair. They both looked up as I came in, the long-legged young man with his villainous black eye, and the old one, too tired to pull himself to his feet. I went towards them, the two people I loved most.